A COLD AWAKENING

Norman Burslem

Best wishes from, Norman & Margaret

ARTHUR H. STOCKWELL LTD
Torrs Park, Ilfracombe, Devon, EX34 8BA
Established 1898
www.ahstockwell.co.uk

British Library Cataloguing-in-Publication Data.
A catalogue record for this book is available
from the British Library.

By the same author:
Family Ways – Austin McCauley, 2017
Nits and Other Afflictions – Arthur H. Stockwell Ltd, 2017
Circle of Life – Forward Poetry, 2018
3 Novum – Novum Publishing gmbh, 2018
5 Novum – Novum Publishing gmbh, 2019
Residual Waste – Arthur H. Stockwell Ltd, 2019

ISBN 978-0-7223-4974-8
Printed in Great Britain by
Arthur H. Stockwell Ltd
Torrs Park Ilfracombe
Devon EX34 8BA

PART ONE: ON THE WAY OUT

CHAPTER 1

One of the many things that irritated Joe Fenton was sitting in the waiting room of his doctor's surgery. He was only here today because his wife had kept on nagging him about a mole which she said had changed shape.

Hitherto in his life Joe had enjoyed mainly good health, and it had been many months since his last visit to see his general practitioner. Today things were obviously running behind schedule, and to make matters worse there were two young children also waiting; both were being fractious, to say the least, but their mothers were unmoved by their cries and shouts; they were involved in a long, animated conversation.

Suddenly one of their mobile phones sprang into life; surprisingly this brought some relief for Joe and the other adult patients in the waiting room because a head appeared over the reception desk and the receptionist uttered a command: "Cancel that call immediately, Miss Clark; mobiles must be switched off at all times in this surgery."

The young woman pulled a face before carrying out the order; her friend tittered after the receptionist had retracted her head.

Above the reception desk there was an electronic screen which announced when one of the three doctors on duty was free to see the next patient. Joe was extremely grateful when his name appeared; he noted he was to see Dr Asmeed; this surprised him because for the last ten years, on his occasional visits to the surgery, he had always been seen by Dr Roger. Joe now went to the reception desk to seek enlightenment.

The receptionist looked up from her screen: "Yes? Can I help you?"

"I hope so. I'm one of Dr Roger's patients, but your device says I'm to see a different doctor."

"Ah yes, I'm afraid Dr Roger is not very well; you see, even those in the medical profession are not immune to the common cold. Dr Asmeed is filling in for him; you'll find her in Dr Roger's consulting room, so please go there quickly because we are very busy today."

The receptionist turned back to her screen, leaving Joe to find his way to the Doctor.

Dr Shula Asmeed looked up from her screen as Joe entered the consulting room.

"Good afternoon, Mr Fenton. Please take a seat."

Joe sat alongside her desk; she was an attractive person, obviously of Asian descent.

"What appears to be the problem, please?"

"Look – I hope I'm not about to waste your time, Doctor, but my wife has been nagging me about a mole I have on my neck. I've had it for years and it has never given me any bother, but Margaret – that's my wife – says it has grown recently and changed colour. I can't really confirm her fears because it's difficult for me to see even in a mirror."

"Your wife is absolutely correct to have pointed out the change, Mr Fenton; now I will take a look."

Joe loosened his tie and undid the top button on his shirt and then turned his head to the right. The Doctor's examination was extremely quick.

"Right, I must refer you immediately to the Dermatology Department at the West Staffordshire Hospital. You will need a biopsy done as soon as possible."

"I'm not in any pain, Doctor."

"Good, but you need expert examination because the mole may now be cancerous."

Joe felt his head reel.

Dr Asmeed tried to lessen his fears: "I can't say it definitely is cancerous, you understand; it may be benign, but it certainly needs checking; a simple biopsy should suffice."

"A what, Doctor?"

"A biopsy. That's where the specialist will take a small fragment of the mole for further examination. Is your wife in the medical profession, by any chance?"

"No."

"Well, she has given you very good advice. Dr Ismael is the main specialist at the West Staffordshire Hospital; he's very experienced and has a fine reputation. You should hear from him within one month; if you don't, please let Dr Roger know. Try not to worry because, as I said earlier, it may be nothing serious."

It was clear to Joe that the consultation was at an end; he fastened his top button, straightened his tie and stood up.

"Thank you, Doctor."

As he drove home Joe decided he would do some research on the Internet; he couldn't think for the life of him that a simple mole could become dangerous, not after all these years. His own mother had first noticed it about forty-five years ago. Joe had had several medical examinations over the years and no medical expert had even mentioned it; no, today, he reckoned, he had been seen by a temporary doctor playing safe. He could understand this: she probably needed the job and money.

By now Joe was approaching his estate on the moors near Cauldon. He and his wife, Margaret, had lived there for fifteen years. The main residence was a spacious bungalow with five bedrooms; there was a stable, which now served as a garage for four vehicles, and an acre of land. Joe's building firm had been very successful and it had long-standing contracts with local authorities and two breweries. Things had turned out fine after an extremely difficult start.

Joe and Margaret had married young and for several years had lived in one of the downmarket areas of Stoke-on-Trent. In those days Joe was a plasterer and Margaret worked in a local supermarket; money had become very tight when their first child had been born, but Joe's boss, old Bert Wilson, had saved the day. He changed his business to a limited company; both Joe and Margaret had become directors, each owning just one share each. But when Bert had retired ten years ago Joe and Margaret had taken over the firm at a time when the local economy was in one of its rare growth periods. Margaret had become Joe's secretary. The couple had kept the business firmly in the family by making their son, Freddie, a director as soon as he was old enough.

The automatic gates opened as Joe drove his Range Rover on to the estate. He knew he would come under intense questioning as soon as he encountered his wife, so he decided to play it cool. He found her in the conservatory.

"How did you get on, Joe? What did Dr Roger say?"

"He wasn't on duty, dear; I saw a locum. She was very good."

"Well, what did she say?"

"Actually she wasn't too sure, so she's arranged for me to see a specialist at the West Staffs Hospital. She didn't think my mole was serious, but a biopsy should confirm a diagnosis."

"What's a biopsy, Joe?"

"Nothing much – they just take a bit of the mole and analyse it. I'm not at all worried, so there is no need for you to fret."

"Joe, you need to go back and see Dr Roger."

"No need for that, dear. Dr Asmeed has put me down for an appointment with a specialist, a Dr Ismael, who, she tells me, is very experienced and has a fine reputation. Now, is there a cup of coffee going?"

His wife left her seat. "Right, I'll get us a drink, but I'd be much happier if you saw Dr Roger."

It was time to change the subject: "Is it tonight Freddie is joining us for dinner?"

"Yes, Joe, and he's bringing his new partner."

Joe had forgotten this fact, but wasn't about to admit it.

"Yes, that's right – of course he is. I hope he makes a go of it this time. Who is she, by the way?"

"She's called Emma; Freddie hasn't told me her surname. I think he met her on one of those dating sites."

"I see. Well, it's better that than on a building site."

Margaret was not amused. "I want you to be polite when you meet her, Joe; we don't want to put her off."

"It's not me who's put off all his other conquests, dear; he seems to have a knack of doing that himself."

Margaret knew that this was true – her son had had many lovers over the decade. She wanted him to settle down and she hoped she would have grandchildren in the very near future.

Joe and Margaret were sipping their coffees in the conservatory when they saw their son's BMW drive on to the estate.

"They're here, Joe."

"Yes, so I see. Now, when he parks let's have a quick shufti at his latest victim."

Freddie got out of the car first; he was an impressive young chap, tall, blond, athletic-looking. He held the door open for Emma. It was obviously a case of opposites attracting, because she was short, dark-haired and older-looking than Freddie.

"Come on, Joe – we'll meet them in the lobby."

Joe obeyed his wife's command.

Freddie and partner were staying for the weekend and this had caused some concerns for Margaret: did they require just one or two bedrooms? She had faced the problem before. The first time Freddie had turned up with a partner there had been embarrassment all round when Margaret had shown the girl of the day to a single bedroom. Today she would use her new plan: she would let Freddie decide which room or rooms the couple would occupy.

"Hi, Mum and Dad. This is Emma."

Both parents smiled at the latest conquest.

"Good afternoon, Emma. Lovely to meet you."

The girlfriend smiled. "It's great to be here, Mrs Fenton – and what a lovely place you have! Freddie described it to me earlier, but it really outdoes his description."

She turned to Joe, who found himself staring at a blue-eyed beauty who was short and shapely.

"Great to meet you, Emma. Now, can I help you with your bags?"

Margaret intervened at this point: "Freddie, you help Emma. Your dad and I will be in the conservatory; we can have an aperitif or two before dinner."

The young couple joined the more mature twosome after twenty minutes or so. Joe had been under strict instructions neither to open the Prosecco until they arrived nor to help himself to the canapés.

"Would you like a glass of fizz, Emma?"

"Yes please, Mr Fenton."

"Oh, call me Joe, Emma – we don't stand on ceremony here."

Margaret supported her spouse for once: "I'm Margaret, Emma. Now, would you like a canapé?"

"Just the one, Margaret, thank you – I'm watching my weight."

"I must do the same, Emma," Margaret assured her, "but I'm sure the men will consume everything; in my experience they usually do."

Her remark caused some slightly strained laughter.

The Prosecco worked its magic – the foursome became more relaxed.

"What do you do for a living, Emma?" Joe enquired.

"I'm training to be an SRN."

Joe was not sure what the abbreviation stood for.

"Emma wants to be a nurse, Dad."

"Oh, right – how's it going, Emma?"

"I'm approaching the end of training now and I've got my fingers crossed."

Over the years Margaret had never developed a means of dealing with alcohol. Today, after two glasses of Italian fizz, her inhibitions were ebbing quickly.

"Emma, could you take a look at the mole on Joe's neck? His doctor wants a specialist to examine it."

Freddie objected: "Mum, we're not here to test Emma; we've come to relax."

Emma did her best to prevent any family row: "It's OK, Freddie – I do know a bit about moles; I'm certainly not an expert, but I can take a look if Joe wants me to."

"No, no, Emma, that would not be an appropriate lead-up to dinner. The Doctor has arranged for me to have a biopsy – she's not particularly worried; I guess she's just covering her back."

Despite his effort Margaret would not let the matter drop: "What happens with a biopsy, Emma?"

"Well, as far as I know, a specialist takes a small sample of the suspect lesion or mole for further analysis; it's a standard procedure and it is not painful."

Joe turned to his wife: "Nothing to worry about, then, Margaret."

His wife wasn't satisfied: "Emma, what can the analysis show up?"

"Well, as Joe has just said, 'nothing serious'."

Margaret still had the lancet in her hand, however: "But there must be other things, Emma."

"Well, yes, but I don't have the knowledge or expertise to

describe Joe's condition; all I can do is to tell you what I have read in my training. A mole can develop into skin cancer, of which there are three broad categories. There is basal cell carcinoma, which is benign although, if left for a long time, it can become malignant; squamous carcinoma is more serious, but, if caught early on in its development, it can be treated successfully. The most serious condition is melanoma, but I believe this too can be eliminated. I guess Joe's doctor wants to find out which type, if any, his mole has developed."

Joe was saved from any further diagnosis because he spotted a van driving on to the estate.

"Dinner has just arrived, folks," he announced.

Margaret changed from inquisitor to hostess: "Oh, good. Now listen, Emma and Freddie – tonight I have ordered a set meal from my and Joe's favourite restaurant. It's called The Olive Tree and its chef is excellent; he specialises in tapas and he's arranged for two of his staff to serve it for us, which means, of course, that we can enjoy the meal uninterrupted."

"Do they do the washing-up as well, Mum?"

"They certainly do, Freddie, so, everyone, let's go to the dining room."

Sometime later everyone agreed the dinner had been excellent; Emma particularly enjoyed a fish dish called *lupina*. She had no idea what the English translation was, but neither did any of her fellow diners. When they had all had enough they retired to the lounge for coffee and digestives.

"Mum, would you mind if I have a quick word with Dad in the study? It's a business matter and I promise we won't be long."

"That's a bit much with your partner here, Freddie."

"I've already mentioned it to her, Mum and she's quite happy."

"Off you go, then, but no more than half an hour."

Once in the study, Joe poured two glasses of Scotch.

"What's the problem, Freddie?"

"No problem, Dad, but an opportunity."

"OK, then, fire away."

"I took a call from a company called Herculeum earlier today; it has planning permission to build a complex of new houses in Chelford and they're looking for a local firm to do the bricklaying and plastering. Now, the bloke I spoke to had done research on our firm; he liked the reviews we've had and our prices. He can offer us a contract for the next eighteen months with the strong possibility of further work in this area, but he needs an answer asap. What do you think?"

"It's a big firm, son, so let's go with it because if things work out well we'll be offered further work I've no doubt."

"I agree, Dad. I'll ring him tomorrow and ask for a draft contract; now we'd better join the ladies or Mum will lose her rag."

CHAPTER 2

The biopsy had been carried out with the minimum of fuss. Joe had attended the Dermatology Department of West Staffordshire Hospital four weeks to the day after his meeting with Dr Asmeed. His only problem had been finding somewhere to park. The procedure had been painless and had lasted a mere ten minutes. Dr Ismael had been chatty and his sense of humour had made Joe laugh at least three times.

Joe had received a letter two weeks later informing him that the result was ready; he had phoned the department to fix an appointment. In view of the parking problems, Joe had asked Margaret to accompany him to ensure he would be on time for the meeting.

"I'll drop you by the main entrance, Joe; then I'll park."

"Fine, Margaret. I'll wait for you in the reception area, but if you're held up finding a parking space you will have to come to the Dermatology Department's waiting area."

Once inside the reception area, Joe signed in on the computer system, which gave him a patient number; he made his way to the dermatology waiting room, where a screen informed him that there was a delay of fifty minutes. All the seats were taken, so Joe propped himself up by a wall and awaited his wife. She turned up half an hour later.

"Have you seen the specialist, Joe?"

"No, dear, there's a delay. Look – there's a couple of seats free at last; let's grab them."

"What's the delay about?"

"I don't know, but we shouldn't be too long."

"Will someone call you?"

"No, I have to wait for my number to come up on that screen over there."

The couple sat in silence and watched the movements of other patients. It soon became clear that some had received disquieting diagnoses. One young woman left the waiting area in tears; an older woman had one arm round her shoulders and was whispering something in her left ear. This couple was followed by a tall, elderly gent who was staring ahead with a worried frown all over his face.

"Your number has come up, Joe."

He looked up at the screen; sure enough the number 1746 was prominently displayed and below it was the room number where the interview would take place.

"Shall I come with you, Joe?"

"I'm not sure if it's allowed, dear, but come anyway. I can ask the Doctor."

Joe knew the way to room eleven. He knocked on the door and immediately heard the specialist's voice: "Come in, Mr Fenton."

Joe popped his head round the door. "Is it OK if my wife joins me?"

Dr Ismael knew he had some potentially upsetting news and, in his extensive experience, he knew spouses were usually, but not always, a supportive influence; it was therefore with some doubt that he answered positively to Joe's request.

"Please sit next to your husband, Mrs Fenton."

Margaret joined her husband, facing the Doctor across his desk.

It was clear from the outset to Joe that today Dr Ismael was in a serious mood; he attempted no jokes or pleasantries apart from the cursory greeting.

"I have the result of your biopsy, Mr Fenton, and I must tell you straight away that you have a problem: your mole has developed a melanoma."

Joe felt his wife's hand grab his.

He attempted to maintain control: "Can you do anything about it, Doctor?"

"Well, it's malignant and it's at stage four out of five; but yes, there are treatments available."

He looked across at Margaret, who, unlike her husband, was

losing control; she had tears in her eyes and she was almost panting.

The Doctor looked directly at her before he spoke again: "I need to question your husband in some depth so I can outline which treatment I consider most appropriate. Please stay if you want to, Mrs Fenton." Margaret nodded, so he turned back to Joe: "I want you to think and then describe any bodily changes you can identify; for instance, do you have any back pain?"

Joe tried to concentrate before answering, but Margaret replied before he did: "He needs to use the toilet more often than he used to, Doctor."

"Is that so, Mr Fenton?"

"Yes, I suppose it is; I need to pee quite often."

"And do you have any problems?"

"Well, the flow seems less than it used to be and sometimes I have a burning sensation in the bladder region."

"That sounds like a prostate-gland problem, so I think you need radiotherapy and chemotherapy, but we must investigate further."

"When can that start, Doctor?"

"Well, Mr Fenton, I'll put you down as an urgent case, so hopefully within a month or so."

Margaret was not happy. "That's far too long, surely."

"Well, you see, Mrs Fenton, the problem is that skin cancer is one of the most common forms of the disease so this department is under constant pressure, but I will do my utmost to make sure your husband receives appropriate treatment as soon as possible."

It was clear to both Fentons that the Doctor needed to move on to his next patient, so, as one, they stood up and left the room.

Once back in the car, Margaret let her emotions rip; she burst into tears immediately she had closed the passenger door.

"Margaret, it's me who has the problem."

"But it's cancer, Joe."

"Yes, I got that, but this is not the time to panic. I have a lot of trust in Dr Ismael and I know that great strides have been made in recent years in the treatment of all forms of cancer; so let's stay positive."

Joe's evaluation of the situation calmed his wife to a degree, but as he drove home she decided she would contact their daughter; surely both their children had to know.

Daughter Valerie had married Arthur Spinks five years ago. They now lived in Harrow, where both had high-paying jobs. Valerie was principal data manager with an educational academy chain and Arthur was employed as a director with a major media company; they were childless so far. Joe and Margaret visited them at their house twice or three times a year; other communication was by email or text and sometimes by phone.

Today Margaret decided that a phone call was the most appropriate because of Joe's diagnosis. She waited till Joe was out in the garden before ringing her daughter.

As usual she did not make immediate contact; a strange voice was in the process of telling her she could leave a message when suddenly Valerie interrupted the system: "Hi, Mum. I can talk."

"Well, thank goodness for that, Valerie."

"Is there a problem, Mum?"

"Yes, with your father: he's been diagnosed with melanoma."

"Oh my God! That's serious, isn't it?"

"Yes, it's a potential killer."

"But he's going to have treatment, I take it."

"Yes, Valerie, but not for a month or so."

"Well, he must go private, Mum; I mean, you have the money."

"Yes, we do, but you know what he's like – he won't want to jump the queue."

"You've got to be firm with him, Mum – he's facing death."

"Could you and Arthur come up here, Valerie, so that we all can try to persuade him?"

"I can, Mum. The school holidays start next week and I'll speak to Arthur; he's busy at the moment, but I'm sure he will do his best."

As Valerie was saying this Margaret heard Joe enter the bungalow.

"I'll ring off now, Valerie – your dad has just come in."

"I can speak to him now, Mum, if you like."

"I think it will be better face-to-face when you visit, Valerie."

"OK, Mum. Goodbye, then, and try not to worry."

Margaret had just put the phone down when Joe entered the kitchen.

"Who was on the blower, dear?"

"Valerie has just rung me, Joe; she can come and visit us next week probably."

"Well, that'll make a change, then; did she say why?"

"No, no; it's just that she's got some time off."

"Is Cocky Sod coming with her?"

"Joe, please don't refer to Arthur like that – he can't help his background."

"Did you tell her about my cancer?"

"Well, no, I thought it better for you to explain person to person; incidentally, when are you going to tell Freddie?"

"I'm thinking about it."

"He'll need to know."

"Of course he'll need to know, but, at the moment, I'm considering when and how I tell him."

Joe decided he needed much more relevant information about his condition before he told both his children. He foresaw that they would ask him many questions, so the more definite answers he had the better.

Joe had turned the smallest bedroom into an office for his sole use.

"I'm just going to my office, Margaret – I need to research a firm which has contacted Freddie with an offer of work."

Margaret made no comment, but was grateful that her husband seemed to be coping well with his melanoma diagnosis.

Once alone, Joe logged on to the Internet and typed 'melanoma' into his search engine. The amount of information available gave him a shock; closer examination revealed that many sites were offering treatment for payment. Joe ignored them and continued his search. Finally he came across the Wikipedia site, which gave objective information about the condition. Joe was particularly interested to read about the Oncofocus test, through which the sequencing of DNA/RNA offered the best match to the most appropriate drugs to combat his condition. Joe felt sure that Dr Ismael would be aware of the test, but he decided to mention it at his next appointment. The information he had gleaned would also help him calm his wife and his children while, at the same time, giving himself some hope.

Next he considered how best to inform Freddie of his condition.

After much thought, he decided to mention his problem at the end of one of their many business discussions, which often took place in a local pub. He looked in his diary and saw he was due to meet Freddie in two days' time. He found his mobile phone and rang his son.

"Hi, Freddie. Look – I wonder if we could bring our next meeting forward to this evening."

"No problem, Dad. In fact I was about to ring you with the same suggestion because we really need a full discussion on the possible contract with Herculeum."

"OK, Freddie. Now, can you meet me later today in The Swan?"

"Sure, Dad, and I'll bring the draft contract. See you later."

Following the call Joe left his office and rejoined his wife in the kitchen.

"I've spoken to Freddie, dear, and I'm meeting him later this evening."

"How did he react, Joe?"

"Well, I didn't give him the full details over the phone; it'll be better face-to-face."

Margaret did not disagree.

CHAPTER 3

Following a normal tense day at his office, Arthur Spinks was looking forward to a calm evening at home. He would have a couple of aperitifs before enjoying one of his wife's delicious dinners accompanied by a bottle of his favourite wine; then he would have a feet-up evening in front of their new smart TV.

When he arrived home, however, Arthur's leisurely expectations were off the table. Valerie was obviously very upset.

"What's wrong, dear?"

"I've had a call from Mum, Arthur – Dad's got skin cancer. She wants us to visit them and try to convince him that he should go private."

"Now hang on a minute, Val – not all skin cancers are life-threatening; I remember my Uncle Horace having something called basal cell carcinoma, which, despite the expressive language, was totally benign."

"He's got melanoma, Arthur."

Arthur was pulled up in his tracks. "Oh" was all he could manage.

"Can we go and see them this weekend, darling?"

Before he answered his wife's question Arthur's memory flashed through his relationship with Joe Fenton. They had never really got on. Joe was a self-made man, born in a poor part of Salford, who had been educated in state schools. After school he was apprenticed to a building firm, where he gained skills in plastering and bricklaying. Arthur, on the other hand, had had a privileged start in life. All his education had been in the private sector and, following study at Bristol University, where he had met Valerie, his father had used contacts to ensure he gained appropriate, highly paid employment after he passed his degree.

Both sets of parents had had considerable problems accepting that Arthur and Valerie should marry. Neither intended spouse met their criteria; nevertheless the marriage went ahead and Arthur's parents had shelled out most of the cash to ensure a suitable ceremony and reception. Arthur did recognise that Joe had lots of business acumen, and this was part of the difficulties both men experienced when forced to communicate with each other. Joe was scornful of Arthur's privileged background. On this occasion, however, Arthur would attempt to be sensitive to his wife's obvious distress.

"Yes, OK, darling, we'll both go."

Later, as he lay in bed, Arthur remembered a company that his firm was negotiating with. The Cryonics Association had entered the field of corpse preservation. This company had had some success in promoting the process in the United States and were now looking to extend their service into the wider world economy. Arthur now considered whether he should mention the process to his father-in-law; he went to sleep with the problem unresolved.

Joe had met Freddie that same day. Freddie had arrived first and was supping a pint of best bitter when his father entered the bar.

"Hi, Dad. I'm over here. Could you get us two pints of best? I'll keep the seats in this alcove."

Joe smiled to himself as he approached the bar – he had trained his son well. It was with some difficulty that he managed to convey the drinks to where Freddie was sitting without spilling a drop.

"Here you are, son."

"Thanks, Dad. Look – I've brought the draft contract with me for you to peruse."

For a moment Joe was confused; Freddie noticed.

"You remember, Dad, that I've been in contact with Herculeum."

Joe now remembered, but he needed to get something off his chest: "Great, Freddie. Now, I must tell you first that I've seen a Dr Ismael at West Staffordshire Hospital; he did a biopsy on my mole and he says I've got skin cancer."

"But you can still work, eh, Dad?"

"Yes, yes, I have a bit of trouble peeing, but a lot of blokes of my age do; anyway, I've probably got to have a minor operation. Now, pass me the contract – I'll study it over the weekend."

"We mustn't hang about, Dad; Herculeum have only given us two weeks to sign up. It's a great deal – it could set us up for years."

Joe smiled at his son and took a swig of his beer.

"Herculeum is a worldwide business, Dad, and it has government contracts here in the UK; association with it could be the making of our firm."

Joe did not disagree.

"OK, Freddie, I understand. Now, to change the subject, Margaret tells me Valerie and Arthur will be with us for the weekend; any chance of you joining us?"

"I can't stand that supercilious twit, Arthur, Dad."

"I'm not too keen either, son, but your mum likes a family get-together."

Freddie knew this to be true.

"I can come for a time on Saturday evening; will it be OK if I bring Lisa?"

"I thought her name was Emma?"

"Oh, sorry, Dad – I forgot to tell you and Mum that Emma and I are no longer an item."

"Your mother does worry, Freddie, that you are not settled; she would like to see you in a stable relationship like your sister."

"There is no female equivalent of Arthur Spinks, Dad – well, not one that I've ever met, thank God."

"Your sister does seem reasonably happy, Freddie."

"Well, good luck to her is all I can say. Right, now I must be going. I'm meeting Lisa – don't forget to read the contract, Dad."

"I won't, son. See you . . ."

The son had left.

Margaret was delighted when Joe told her that Freddie would be able to join the family get-together.

"He's bringing his latest girlfriend, dear," Joe told her.

"Oh, good. I really like Emma – she seems mature and sensible."

"He's given Emma the boot, dear; the new conquest is called Lisa."

"Why on Earth has he ditched Emma, Joe? I really liked her."

"I haven't a clue, Margaret."

"Did you tell him about your diagnosis?"

"Yes, I did mention it, but he's very caught up with a development at work."

"Look, Joe – I'll have a word with him on his own when he's here."

"That might be difficult. You know he always avoids anything to do with kitchens and food preparation."

"Oh, I'll ask him to help me with the drinks. He must come to understand the seriousness of your condition."

"Margaret, listen to me – let's not be too emotional about this just now. I feel OK apart from some pain down below, and Dr Ismael's treatment might sort things out, so let's be low-key. I agree the kids need to know, but let's not scare them at this point in time; I'm feeling positive, so let me take the lead in any discussion. You see, a drip-feed approach helps people come to terms with difficult situations better than a full-blown outpouring."

Margaret paused before agreeing to her husband's ploy. "Well, I hope they take things seriously, Joe."

CHAPTER 4

It was high summer in the Staffordshire moorlands, and surprisingly it hadn't rained for a fortnight. Joe had formed a plan for the family get-together: he would organise a barbecue and he would do the cooking. This, he hoped, would spare him from emotional exchanges with his daughter and wife. Margaret had not been keen on the plan, but she had finally agreed although somewhat reluctantly.

The estate had a large patio which extended from the lounge; beyond it the swimming pool looked very inviting on this warm summer evening. Joe had set up the barbecue away from the pool and the seating area; he was wearing his special apron, which sported a pattern dedicated to Stoke City Football Club, together with a chef's hat. He had designated Margaret to supervise the drinks. He hoped that his tactics would lessen the opportunities for his daughter to interrogate him about his health and for his son to rabbit on about business matters.

Margaret met the guests when they arrived. Two large, expensive vehicles drove on to the estate within minutes of each other. Valerie was the first to emerge from the BMW SUV.

"Where's Dad, Mum?"

"We're having a barbecue, darling – your dad's cooking the burgers."

"I was hoping to have a chat with him on his own."

"Well, that may be possible after we've eaten, Valerie."

Valerie was now joined by her husband, who had parked their vehicle.

"Good evening, Margaret. Long time no see. How are you?"

"I'm OK, Arthur, but I'm very worried about Joe."

She got no further because her son's Porsche, which had raced up the drive, had now skidded to a halt on the loose gravel parking area. The threesome in attendance watched as two doors opened almost simultaneously; all eyes were drawn to Freddie's latest acquisition. She was tall, blond and shapely.

"Hiya, everyone. This is Julie." Freddie called out the introduction.

Julie smiled as she approached. Margaret expected her to speak in an educated tone, but she was disappointed.

"Hiya, folks." Julie's greeting definitely had the local intonation. "Ta for inviting me," she added.

Margaret was about to pour the drinks, but the arrival of another vehicle stopped her in her tracks.

She turned to the guests: "Does anyone know who this is?"

Freddie recognised the male who was extricating himself from the driver's side.

"It's Rodney Salt from work, Mum."

"Have you invited him, Freddie? Because if you have I shall be very cross; this is supposed to be a family event to support Joe?"

"Honest, Mum, it wasn't me."

Freddie was not always truthful, but today he was innocent because his father had invited his old pal and workmate, Rodney Salt. Rodney came stumbling towards them; he was obese and he was smoking. Joe had invited him so he could have an excuse for avoiding any emotional outbursts from his daughter – or anybody else, for that matter.

He called out to his old friend: "Over here, Rod. Maggie will bring us a beer."

Margaret did not enjoy hosting surprise guests and she hated being referred to as Maggie.

Freddie now took the opportunity to help his mother: "I'll take them a beer, Mum, and I'll have one for myself." He turned to his latest catch: "You wait here, Julie – I won't be long. Have a chat with Valerie and Arthur."

When he left there was an awkward silence, finally broken by Valerie: "Do you live locally, Julie?"

"Yes, in Chelford; that's where I met Freddie."

"Do you work in the town, then?"

"Yes, at the supermarket."

Arthur decided to join the interrogation: "Are you management?"

"No, duck, I'm on the checkout; Freddie and I got talkin' and he invited me out."

"So, how long have you known him?" Valerie wanted to know.

"Oh, for more than a fortnight – he's a real laugh."

Margaret joined the trio: "Here we are, everyone – nibbles and an aperitif."

All concerned were grateful for the interruption. It was time to nibble and sup slowly.

Freddie had poured three beers while Margaret was preparing the more upmarket selection.

"Freddie, go and remind your father that this is a family occasion."

Joe knew all about family occasions and how they could deteriorate into strife, but at this moment he had a bladder problem. He looked up from his sizzling burgers.

"Rod, I need a pee – look after this lot for me, will you?"

"Sure, Joe."

"I'm 'aving a bit of bother in the bladder department at the moment, Rod."

"Yeah, me too. Now, what I do is this: I put my left 'and under me scrotum and I push upwards into the bollocks; it works every time. Mind you, I need a mop and bucket handy."

Joe did not hear all the detail of the possible cure – the nearest toilet beckoned.

Freddie arrived with the drinks: "I've brought us some beer, Rod."

"Good lad. Joe's just been telling me about his bladder problem."

"Oh yeah, but don't worry – he's having treatment. You've heard about the contract with Herculeum, I take it."

"Yeah, brilliant. It should set our firm up for bloody years."

"That's right, Rod, and it should make us a shedload of dosh."

Margaret's arrival prevented any more acclamations: "Where's your father, Freddie?"

Rod answered her: "He's just nipped to the little boys' room, Maggie."

"Did he invite you to this family gathering, Rodney?"

"Well, yeah. He said, 'Pop in, we're 'aving a barbecue.'"

"I'm only asking because this evening we do need an urgent family discussion, you see."

"Oh, right, OK, I'll just finish this beer and I'll be off."

"Thank you so much, Rodney." Margaret now turned to her son: "Freddie I want you and your latest partner to take over here when Joe returns."

"I'm useless at cooking, Mum."

"Yes, I know that, darling, but I'm sure what's-her-name will be fine, so invite her to take charge and then you join Valerie, Arthur and me."

The group around the barbecue broke up. Margaret and Freddie returned to the family members; Rod downed his beer quickly. He was sensitive enough to know when he wasn't welcome.

Once back with Valerie and Arthur, Freddie took Julie to one side: "Could you just watch the barbecue for a couple of minutes, love? I need to keep Mum sweet."

Julie smiled at her lover. "I like doing barbecues, Fred."

Margaret, however, was not so happy. "Where on Earth is your father, Freddie?"

"Rod told you, Mum – he's in the bog."

"Don't use language like that, Freddie, please."

Arthur was now feeling distinctly uncomfortable. "Look – I know you need to talk to Joe about his health, so, if you like, I'll go and find him then help Julie with the food."

Margaret was grateful: "Oh, thank you, Arthur."

His wife was not so contented: "Arthur, please don't touch anything that's cooking."

"Especially not Julie, eh, Arthur?"

Arthur forced a grin at Freddie's intended joke and left in the direction of the barbecue and the toilets.

Joe had only managed a trickle despite the fact his bladder felt full; he tried Rodney's suggestion without any success and he was surprised when he heard someone tap on the toilet door.

"I haven't finished yet; you'll have to use the toilet in the main bathroom," he shouted.

He received a second surprise when he heard Arthur's voice: "The family wants a word with you, Joe."

"Is the food ready, then?"

"Yes, I think so."

Reluctantly Joe opened the door.

"Is everything all right, Joe?"

"Well, apart from a loss of pressure, yes, thank you."

"My Uncle Richard suffered from prostate cancer. That was years ago, of course; there are much better treatments these days. Have you heard about oncology?"

"I found something online that mentioned it, but it didn't mean anything much to me."

"Well, I'm not a medical expert either, Joe, but I understand that greater knowledge of DNA and RNA allows the medics to sort out less intrusive treatments."

"Really?"

"Why don't you ask your specialist about them?"

"OK, I'll do that. Now, let's get eating. I hope Rod hasn't messed up the barbecue."

"Oh, he's left, Joe. I saw him drive off a few minutes ago."

"Bloody 'ell! I specifically asked him to keep his eye on the grub."

"I don't think you need worry, Joe – Freddie's young lady has taken over."

"Oh my God! Come on – let's get over there."

Julie was in her element; she loved cooking either indoors or, like today, outdoors.

"I'm going to use some of this Farmer's BBQ Bovine Bold Rub. We use it at 'ome – it's brilliant."

"I'll stay and help you, Julie, because I know Margaret wants a chat with Joe while their two children are around."

As if to confirm Arthur's statement, Margaret's voice penetrated every eardrum: "Joe, come over here, please. We all want a word with you!"

Joe made sure he had his glass of beer as he joined his wife and children on the patio.

Margaret took the lead: "Joe, we've all given plenty of thought to your problem and we all think you need to go private; as you know, money is not a problem."

Valerie sought to back her mother: "With cancer, Dad, time is of the essence. The sooner it's treated the better."

Freddie joined in: "And, Dad, we need you fully fit at work, what with this new contract and everything."

Joe took a big swig from his glass, breathed in and then stuck his chest out.

"Now, all of you, listen to me. I've done research online and I've found out that there are many treatments available for melanoma. What's more, my specialist is excellent; I have every trust in him. There is a system called oncology which targets the essential cancer cells. Arthur knows about the system – in fact, we were discussing it a few minutes ago."

"Does your specialist know about this oncology thing, Dad?"

"Of course he will, Valerie. Look – there is no need to panic. I'm seeing Dr Ismael soon; he will have the results from my latest tests and he'll have a course of treatment ready to go. Now, come on – let's all enjoy the grub."

As if to confirm everything Joe had just explained, Julie's voice caught everyone's attention: "The food's ready!"

CHAPTER 5

It was going to be a scorching summer day. Dr Sachin Ismael had arrived early in the Dermatology Department. His family was of South Asian origin, but he himself had been born in Birmingham – a town not noted for overpowering heat. He knew he had a tough day ahead; his first appointment was at 8 a.m. and, apart from a thirty-minute break for lunch, he was due to see his last patient at seven that evening. What was more, he had some disturbing diagnoses for several people.

He knew from past experience that patients' reactions could vary considerably when they heard their prognosis. He always sought to give some hope, but that was not always possible; today, for instance, he had to tell Joe Fenton that his cancer had spread into his lymphatic system so that his life expectancy was limited. He would of course explain that palliative care would lessen any suffering, but even such news could induce extreme reactions. Some patients were totally stunned; others went immediately into denial; others still blamed the health service for the problem. Dr Ismael also knew, however, that he must be truthful. Over the years he had learned how to remain totally objective, and he always did his best to control his own emotions; this was particularly difficult with young patients. Some elderly patients accepted their situation; a few had even thanked him for his explanations.

Nurse Sumitri Khan entered his surgery at seven thirty.

"Good morning, Doctor. I believe we have a very busy day ahead."

"Yes indeed, Nurse. When we start please sit behind the patients, but keep in my eyeline. If I nod my head come and sit alongside me so you can intervene in support."

"Of course, Doctor. It has worked in the past – not perfectly every time, of course, but any patient who is overcome I will take to the room next door and attempt to calm them before they leave. That should help you keep to the appointment times."

Sachin was grateful that he had such experienced support on this particular day. Nurse Khan always collected patients from the waiting room and passed the time of day with them as she led them to the surgery; this also helped promote a calm atmosphere, at least at the start of the consultation.

"Nurse, I've got some difficult news for Mr Joseph Fenton. I do hope his wife is not with him; she became very upset at an earlier consultation, so you may have to direct your support more to her. I reckon Mr Fenton might go into denial."

"Right, Doctor. Shall I go and see if our first patient has arrived?"

"Yes, please, Nurse. Let's make a punctual start at least."

Dr Ismael was not the only one who was worried about Margaret Fenton's reactions – so was her husband, Joe. He had kept the news of his latest consultation from her as long as possible. He was delighted when he overheard her on the phone fixing a lunch date with her old friend Freda Tanner on the same day as his appointment. He held off telling her about it for two more days.

At dinner on Wednesday evening he made an announcement: "Margaret, I've got my appointment at the hospital; it came today."

"When is it for, Joe?"

"This Friday at eleven thirty."

"Well, that's not much warning, is it?"

"No, but probably someone has cancelled, so they've fitted me in."

"Oh hell, Joe, I've arranged to meet Freda for lunch on Friday."

"Don't worry, dear – I can go alone, no sweat."

"But the parking, Joe – you know what it's like."

"I've given that a lot of thought: now, I'll park at the nearby supermarket. I can have two and half hours free – that should be plenty of time."

"But it's miles away, Joe."

"No it isn't – it's fifteen minutes on foot, that's all. Look – I don't want to mess up your lunch date."

"Well, ring me on your mobile when you get out."

"Good idea, dear – I'll do that."

After they had eaten Joe went to his office; Margaret took the opportunity to ring her daughter using her mobile.

"Valerie, it's Mum here; your dad told me earlier that his next appointment is this coming Friday."

"Well, that's not much notice, Mum. Are you accompanying him?"

"I wanted to, Valerie, but I've got a dinner date with my old friend Freda and Joe has insisted that I keep to the arrangement; he'll phone me though when he's seen the Doctor."

"How's he been, Mum, since the barbecue?"

"He visits the toilet a lot – several times at night – and he says he keeps having tummy trouble. I've told him to keep off the booze."

"Well done, Mum. Now are you going to phone Freddie?"

"I think I'll leave it, Valerie – you know what he's like. He's only really interested in work and girlfriends, and if he tries to intervene he could complicate things further."

"Look, Mum – when you find out Dad's latest results give me a ring. I'll have to phone off now – Arthur's due any minute, you see."

Margaret did see; she understood that children's priorities could be split as they got older.

As usual the waiting area at the Dermatology Department was completely full. Joe was quite out of breath when he arrived; his walk from the supermarket parking lot had been quite a challenge. He leaned on a wall as he waited his turn; he made sure he could see the large screen so that he could move immediately his number came up.

"Mr Fenton, please."

Joe was surprised when a nurse came into the waiting area and called his name.

"Yes, I'm here."

"Oh good. Dr Ismael will see you in room thirteen."

'Well, that's not a happy omen,' Joe thought to himself as he followed Nurse Khan.

"Have you found somewhere to park, Mr Fenton?"

"Yes, thank you, Nurse – I've left my car at the supermarket."

"Good idea, Mr Fenton. Actually many of the staff, including myself, have difficulty finding a space; the hospital trust really needs to get it sorted. Right, we're nearly there; please take a seat opposite Dr Ismael."

Once inside room thirteen, Joe took the correct seat; he was surprised though that the Nurse sat behind him a little to his left.

Dr Ismael looked up from his screen and smiled. "Good morning, Mr Fenton. Now, before I tell you the results of your tests I'd like to know how you've been since our last meeting."

Joe considered his response for a second or two.

"Not too bad, Doctor. I'm still having a few problems passing urine; I've sometimes had a backache and for the last couple of weeks I've had a bit of indigestion. I'm getting on a bit, so I suppose I must expect these things."

Dr Ismael was not smiling any more. "I have the results here from your most recent tests." He paused and looked up from his screen, because he wanted to judge Joe's reaction so far. His patient looked calm enough, so he continued: "The analysis shows that the cancer has spread into your lymphatic system, which, as I am sure you know, connects with all parts of the body, including the important organs. Your problem urinating, for instance, shows us that the cancer is affecting your prostate gland and the backache indicates problems with your kidneys. Now, your tummy ache could well be a sign of pancreatic cancer; I shall need to do more tests to make absolutely sure."

Joe did his best to maintain some control of his emotions. "It sounds like a mess, Doctor," he said with a forced smile.

Dr Ismael did not smile back. "Your condition is very serious, Mr Fenton."

"How serious?"

Sachin Ismael nodded his head before replying, and Joe heard some movement from behind his left side; the Nurse came to sit next to the Doctor.

The Doctor's next words caused a cold sweat for the patient: "Life-threatening, I'm afraid, Mr Fenton."

A whirl of confusion span in Joe's mind.

"Can't you do anything?"

The Nurse answered his question: "Oh yes, we can instigate palliative care."

It was clear to both doctor and nurse that Joe Fenton was now even more confused, but he did manage his own question: "What about oncology? My son-in-law tells me it's the latest step forward."

Dr Ismael took up the explanation: "Yes, Mr Fenton, we have used that technique, but unfortunately your cancer is too embedded and too widespread."

"What if I go private? I've got the money."

"Of course you can do that, but there are no other treatments, even in the private sector, so you will be told exactly the same as I am telling you today. Now, would you like—"

The Doctor was about to suggest that Nurse Khan should have a private chat with Joe about palliative care, but Joe interrupted him: "How long have I got?"

"Well, it's difficult to give an exact time, but about a year."

"Bloody 'ell."

Nurse Khan tried to calm Joe: "If you come with me now, Mr Fenton, I'll explain our palliative methods; I think the Doctor will agree that we can solve your prostate problem using the latest breakthrough."

Sachin Ismael did agree. "Yes indeed, Nurse. Our treatment can be carried out under local anaesthetic and you'll be able to go home the same day. I'll put you down for an early intervention. Now, if you go with Nurse Khan she will give you full details of our palliative care."

Joe stood up; he had had too much information.

"I've got to go."

He turned to leave, but Nurse Khan tried to dissuade him: "I'm sure you'll feel happier when you hear our system, Mr Fenton."

Joe ignored her and left room thirteen.

"Be careful as you drive," the Doctor called after him.

Once in his car, Joe's emotions overpowered him; tears ran down his cheeks and he gasped for breath. Some minutes later he remembered he should phone Margaret, but he couldn't face the call; instead he rang his old friend Rodney Salt.

"Rod, do you fancy a pint?"

"Yeah, OK, Joe. Is everything all right?"

"I'll tell you when we meet. You know that pub The Swan in Chelford High Street – I'll meet you there in twenty minutes."

"Fine, Joe. See you there."

Strangely enough Joe found that driving his car helped calm his nerves and he arrived at the pub within fifteen minutes; Rod's vehicle was nowhere to be seen, so he parked up and entered the building. The Swan was now owned by a national chain; it had a bar, a restaurant and an outside smoking area. Joe had been trying to give up cigarettes, but today he needed something to help calm his emotions; he sat in the outside area and lit up. Rod joined him ten minutes later.

"Hi, Joe. Hey, what's this? I thought you were off the weed."

Joe forced a smile; Rod could see there was something big amiss.

"I'll get us a couple of pints, Joe."

When he returned Joe's cigarette was snuffed out.

"Here's a pint, Joe. Chin-chin."

Rod sat down opposite his friend. He didn't really know what to say, so he took large sips from his beer; Joe left his untouched.

Rod tried to open the conversation: "What do you think of Stoke City's latest?" He got no further.

Joe opened up: "I've got cancer, Rod."

"Oh."

"They tell me I've only got a year left."

"Left for what, Joe?"

"Fucking life."

"Who's told you this, Joe?"

"The bloody specialist."

"Come on – I mean they can cure loads of cancers these days."

"Well, they can't bloody well cure mine; all they can offer is palliative care."

"Pally what, Joe? That sounds friendly."

Rod's intended joke foundered on the rock of his friend's anguish. Joe lowered his head; a choking sound came through his lips.

Rod tried a different tack: "God, that's terrible, Joe! Does the family know?"

Joe lifted his glass and took a heavy swig before answering: "They know I have a problem, but not this latest diagnosis."

"You'll have to tell them, Joe."

"I know I'll have to fucking tell them, but how and when?"

Rod made no attempt to solve this problem; instead he finished his beer.

"Would you like another pint, Joe?"

Joe didn't answer verbally, but he merely waved his glass at his friend.

Margaret's lunch date with her old friend had not gone well because Margaret was not concentrating on either the conversation or the food.

"What's wrong, Margaret?" Finally Freda asked the appropriate question.

"Joe's not well and he's getting some test results about now."

"What seems to be wrong with him, Margaret?"

"It's cancer, Freda."

Her friend had sought to lessen her worries: "There have been big advances in treatments, Margaret; many are successful as long as the problem is tackled in time."

This last phrase had added to Margaret's concern. After coffee she had made her excuses and left the café. She was becoming more and more agitated. She had not had a call from her husband; she had tried phoning and texting him. Both had failed. Surely he wasn't still at the hospital. Of course there may have been a long delay and she knew that he couldn't have his phone on while in the building. She waited another half-hour before trying again.

She received no response, so this time she left a voicemail message: "Joe, it's Margaret. Please get in touch; I'm worried sick."

Margaret remained worried sick for another half-hour or so. When she arrived home her agitation was such that she needed to speak to someone desperately; she phoned Valerie from her home landline.

"It's me, darling. I'm really worried about Joe – he's been at the hospital for hours and he hasn't let me know a thing."

Valerie was also under pressure: she had to attend an important meeting in the next half-hour.

"There's probably a delay in the Dermatology Department, Mum. You know what it's like these days – not enough staff to cope. But, as the old saying goes, no news is good news. Now, I must ring off, but I'll speak to you later; try ringing Freddie."

Margaret followed her daughter's suggestion. Her son's mobile was active and he answered immediately, but she received no immediate support.

"Sorry, Mum – I'll have to speak to you later; I'm in a meeting with a director from Herculeum."

At The Swan the beer continued to flow. Rod was well aware that both he and Joe were well over the drink-drive limit.

"When do you want to leave, Joe, only we've drunk quite a few?"

"I'll be all right, Rod. It doesn't matter if I have a prang – the quicker I go the better."

"I should ring your wife, Joe; I'm sure she'll understand."

"She bloody won't; she'll say everything is my fault. Now I need the bog again."

Joe stood up shakily and wobbled his way into the bar; Rod took the opportunity to ring Joe's home number on his mobile.

"Hello. Is that Maggie? It's Rod Salt here. I'm with Joe at The Swan; we've both had a few—"

"Is he all right, Rodney? I've been worried sick."

"Well, we're both a little tipsy. Could you come and give us a lift to your place? I'll get a taxi home from there."

"Yes, yes, I'll come. Now can I speak to Joe, please?"

"He's in the bog – I mean the gents."

"Wait there, Rodney and don't let him drive off; he's lost his licence before." She rang off.

Joe had left his jacket draped on the back of his chair; Rod searched his pockets and found his car key, which he put in his own trouser pocket just before Joe returned to the table.

"Still can't pee properly. Now I've got to be off." He lifted his jacket from the chair back. "Where are my bloody keys? I could swear I left them in my jacket."

"Perhaps you've dropped them, Joe. Why don't you go back to the bog to see if they're on the floor?"

Joe did not take up his friend's suggestion; instead he sat

back down again, head in hands.

Rod didn't know how to react, but he was saved from further awkwardness because Margaret had arrived; Rod could see her looking round the bar. He waved to her.

"Maggie is here, Joe."

Joe remained as he was, completely uncommunicative. Rod went to meet her.

"He's in the smoking area, Maggie. I've got to go to the gents; I'll join you in a couple of minutes."

Margaret pushed past him.

"Joe, I'm here. What on Earth is wrong and why didn't you phone me?"

Her husband raised his head; he opened his mouth, but no words came out.

"Joseph Fenton, you've been drinking. Now, what did they tell you at the hospital?"

This time Joe managed a short reply: "I've got to have a minor op on my prostate."

"Well, that sounds all right to me, and surely it's no reason to get drunk."

Margaret would have said more, but Rod's return ensured her silence.

"I've found your keys, Joe. You dropped them in the gents."

Rod handed the keys to his friend, who frowned at him but said nothing.

Margaret took the initiative: "Come on, you two drunks – I'll drive you home, but first you'd better explain to the manager that you'll pick your cars up tomorrow."

Like two naughty schoolboys, Joe and Rod followed Margaret back into the bar and then to the parking area.

CHAPTER 6

Margaret awoke with a start. What on Earth was that noise? She turned to wake her husband; he wasn't lying next to her.

"Joe, where are you?"

She received no reply. She left the bed and opened the en-suite door – there was no sign of her husband. She left the bedroom. Once outside on the landing, she heard a groan. She rushed to the main bathroom, where she found Joe crumpled on the floor. He groaned again.

"Joe, darling, what's wrong?"

"I need 'elp. Ring 999 quickly."

Despite her confusion and her need for answers, Margaret went back into the bedroom and dialled.

"I need an ambulance; my husband's collapsed and he's in a terrible state." She gave her address and then returned to the bathroom.

Joe lay there on his left side with his knees pressed into his chest; he was moaning softly. Quickly Margaret took off her nightdress and put on some outdoor clothes. Ten minutes later the ambulance arrived.

She told the medics all she knew about Joe's problem: "I know he's got prostate cancer and a melanoma; he's been told he needs an operation for his prostate."

"Right, we'll get him to A & E; it sounds as though his urethra is fully blocked."

"Can I come too?"

"Yes, and please keep talking to him as we drive; I'll monitor his condition on the way, so I can give whoever is on duty the data. Bring a mobile phone if you have one so you can ring a family member when we know an outcome. Of course, you'll have to do that outside the hospital building."

They arrived at the hospital less than half an hour later. Joe's condition meant that a doctor came to examine him within minutes; Margaret was able to tell her all she knew about the urinary problem.

"He's one of Dr Ismael's patients, you say, Mrs Fenton. Right, first I'll empty his bladder, then I'll check his hospital record; I suggest you stay in the waiting area. I'll report back to you quite soon, I hope."

By now Margaret was feeling a little calmer. She looked at her watch – it was almost midnight. She thought about the day's events. Why hadn't Joe phoned her from the hospital? Perhaps he was holding something back! So she decided to ring Rodney Salt; she knew that Rodney always stayed up late.

A male answered her call almost immediately: "Who is this? If it's a scam you'd better bloody watch—"

Margaret interrupted him: "It's Margaret here, Rodney. Joe has been rushed into theatre."

"Oh my God! He's not on his last legs, is he?"

"No, but why do you ask that question?"

"Earlier today, while we were in the pub, Joe told me that he had only a short time to live – you know, what with the cancer and that."

The information shut Margaret up; once again confusion raged in her mind.

"Are you still there, Maggie?"

"Yes, but who told Joe?"

"That specialist of 'is: I forget 'is name."

A blinding flash of horror hit Margaret. Rodney was telling the truth: Dr Ismael had revealed the true picture of Joe's condition; Joe had not been able to tell her. He had reverted to his old ways – share it with a friend before her. There had been other instances in the past when she had been the last to be informed of major events by her husband. She ended the call; it was time to contact the children.

She was about to dial Valerie, but the Doctor interrupted her: "We are draining your husband's bladder now, Mrs Fenton. It's a

37

simple procedure, but I'll need to keep him in the hospital for a day or two. Now I've had chance to read his notes and I'm sure you know how serious his condition is; I've left a message for Dr Ismael and I've no doubt he'll contact you early tomorrow. Are you all right, Mrs Fenton? Look – have a seat."

Margaret slumped backwards on to a chair.

"You do know about your husband's condition, don't you?"

Margaret managed to look up at her questioner. "I found out this evening; his best friend has just told me."

The Doctor was clearly perturbed by this revelation. "Oh, I'm so sorry."

"His friend told me a few minutes ago that Joe found out earlier today, but he didn't let me know."

The Doctor sat beside her and took her hand. "People react in many different ways to such news, Mrs Fenton. Do you have children, by any chance?"

"Yes."

"Well, I strongly suggest you ring them now."

Dr Craven would have stayed with Margaret, but a nurse appeared.

"You're needed for triage, Dr Craven."

Valerie or Freddie? Margaret, as always, chose her daughter first.

She dialled the number and waited while Valerie's phone rang; then a strange voice spoke: "The person you have called is not—"

A second voice interrupted the first: "Is that you, Mum?"

"Yes, Valerie, I'm at the general hospital; your father has been admitted."

"Oh dear – what's wrong?"

Margaret had maintained some composure up to this point, but now she was overcome; Valerie heard her obvious distress.

"Mum, please, what's wrong?"

"He's dying, Valerie. Can you come to the hospital right now?"

Her daughter didn't answer her; instead Margaret heard another voice in the background.

Arthur spoke to her next: "I'm sorry to have to ask you this, Margaret, but is he dying as we speak?"

"No, he's had an operation to ease his bladder problem, but he is very seriously ill."

Margaret heard another conversation in the background before Valerie spoke again: "Are they keeping him in hospital, Mum?"

"Yes, for a day or two."

Arthur was back on the line: "Right, Margaret, we'll come to see you, then, on Saturday. As you know, it's a long drive and we both have to arrange things at work. Now I suggest you ring Freddie; he's local and I'm sure he can get to you in the next half-hour, so I'll ring off to let you call him. Please ring us back after you've spoken to him. Bye for now."

Margaret lowered her mobile to find her son's number, but she was interrupted by a member of staff: "I'm sorry, madam, but you must not ring from here; I must ask you to leave this area and phone from outside."

Margaret looked up at the man, who was clearly a member of the security staff. "My husband is dying; I need support."

"I'm very sorry, but your mobile could interfere with our systems. Let me show you the best place to ring from."

Margaret stood up and followed him. Once under the outside awning, she tapped in Freddie's number. Once again there was a long wait before someone picked up.

"Freddie, it's me. Your dad is in hospital – he's very ill. Can you come, please?"

Freddie did not answer her straight away; Margaret heard him speak to someone else. This time she could understand some of Freddie's conversation.

"It's my mum, love. My dad's in hospital; she wants me to go."

Margaret could not discern the reply; no doubt it was a young woman.

At last, after what seemed like an epoch, Freddie addressed her: "I'll get to you soon, Mum; I've just got to drop off a friend on the way. She's got no transport, see."

Margaret did see and she understood that for both her children their father's health and her own need for support were not their immediate top priorities.

Dr Craven rejoined her.

"The procedure was successful, Mrs Fenton. Your husband is sleeping peacefully, so I suggest you return home and try to get some sleep so you can return here somewhat refreshed when he wakes up. Have you got transport?"

"My son is on his way, Doctor."

"Good. I'll say goodbye, then, and hope to see you again soon."

Freddie arrived at the hospital one hour later. He found his mother slumped in a chair in the corridor.

"What's happened, Mum? Why has Dad been admitted?"

"Sit here next to me, Freddie."

Her son did as she requested. Margaret looked across at him.

"Earlier today, Freddie, your dad was told that he has only a little time left to live. This evening he collapsed at home and I called an ambulance."

"Is he dying now, Mum?"

"No, he has a prostate problem, which the hospital has sorted for a short time, but he has been told he has probably only one year of life left."

Freddie Fenton was not often stuck for words, but tonight was different.

"Have you nothing to say, Freddie?"

Her son pursed his lips and blew out some air, then he posed a question: "So he won't be able to work, then?"

"Really, Freddie, is that the most important aspect of your dad – his ability to work?"

"Well, no, but he's got to sign a contract with Herculeum; it means a lot to him."

"And to you also, no doubt, but I'm sure your dad will be able to sign his name when he wakes up; now I need some sleep, so take me home, please."

CHAPTER 7

Valerie Spinks slept very badly after hearing the news about her father. At 4 a.m. she got up and went downstairs to make a cup of tea. While she was waiting for the kettle to boil she was joined by her husband.

"I thought I'd heard you get up, Valerie."

"I can't sleep, Arthur; the news about Dad is absolutely terrible. Really I ought to be on my way now to join her."

"Oh, I'm sure Freddie will have done the honours."

As if to back up her husband's opinion, Valerie's mobile rang; it was Margaret.

"Freddie's brought me home, Valerie, and he's staying the night – or what's left of it – here at the estate."

"That's good, Mum. I'm sure you need some rest. Look – ring me tomorrow, at work if need be, to let me know how Dad is. I'm free in the morning."

"I doubt whether I'll sleep, Valerie, but I'll give it a go. Goodbye for now."

Valerie switched off her mobile; her husband was deep in thought.

"Are you OK, Arthur?"

"I've just remembered that my firm is negotiating a contract with an American organisation."

"Really, Arthur! Just at the moment there are more important things than your damn job."

"Just hold on a second, Val. The American firm is called The Cryonics Association; now I'm not directly involved, but there may be some hope for your father."

"Ridiculous! How can a bunch of Yanks help save my dad?"

"Do you know anything about cryonics, Val?"

"No."

"Then you need to listen: cryonics, as I understand it, is a way of revitalising people who have died; it involves freezing the person's body immediately after death so that, when medical science has progressed enough, persons can be brought back to life when there are renewal treatments to cure whatever killed them. Now, I don't know everything about the process, but tomorrow I can chat to my colleague who is involved with the Americans, to find out more. There might be some hope for your father, and that may help your mother too."

Valerie had to admit to herself that her husband might have something to offer, although she doubted that there was any future for her father.

"I'll mention it to Mum tomorrow, Arthur, and tell her that by Saturday we may have fuller details."

Margaret returned to the hospital alone the following morning. Dr Craven was off duty, but Dr Ismael had found a few minutes to speak to her.

"Your husband is awake, Mrs Fenton. He can come home later today and I'll arrange help for you. We can't keep him in because there is a tremendous demand for beds. Would you like to see him now?"

"Yes please, Doctor."

Joe was sitting up in bed in a male ward.

"How are you, Joe? You gave me a real scare last night."

"They've strapped a bag to my left thigh; it's there to collect my pee." It was clear from Joe's expression that he wasn't very happy.

Margaret tried to mitigate his depression: "Well, at least your bladder won't get blocked like it did last night."

Joe merely grunted.

Margaret now attempted to change the subject: "Freddie looked after me last night, and Valerie and Arthur are coming at the weekend; you'll be there to meet them."

Neither piece of information made any obvious difference to Joe's negative attitude.

"When can I get out of here?"

"Later today, Joe. Dr Ismael is fixing some support for us."

As if to back up Margaret's information a nurse appeared at his bedside.

"I just need to empty your bag, Mr Fenton; I'll show you how to do it, so you can manage it yourself when you get home later today. Please excuse us, Mrs Fenton."

Margaret took the hint: "Right, Joe, I'll return home now to prepare for your return and I'll let Freddie know; I'm sure he'll come to see you after work."

Arthur Spinks had arranged a meeting with his work colleague Sonny Rawlings.

"Come into my office, Sonny, and have a pew."

Sonny did as requested and lowered his two-metre height on to an office chair beside Arthur's desk.

"I'd like a chat with you, Sonny, about The Cryonics Association."

Arthur's colleague frowned. "Now, hang on a moment, Arthur – cryonics is my show."

"Yes, yes, I know that, and I'm not trying to inveigle my way in; it's just that my father-in-law is on his last legs – he's got cancer and he'll be dead within the year. Now, as I understand it, cryonics can offer an opportunity to bring the dead back to life sometime in the future." Arthur raised both eyebrows to signify a question, but he didn't receive a quick answer.

Sonny lowered his head and contemplated. He was negotiating with the American firm, who wanted to invest in Europe and beyond. They had money, know-how and equipment; what they wanted now was dying person. Arthur's relative could be ideal. Sonny looked up.

"Yeah, that's right, Arthur. The cryonics system could spread across the world."

"What is the process, then, Sonny?"

"I'm meeting Kenneth Steinberg later this morning. He's a director of The Cryonics Association. We're close to an agreement whereby we will advertise and promote his firm, and of course what we really need is a dead body – a fresh one."

"Have you approached anyone so far, Sonny?"

"Nope, but if I can mention your dying relative that could

be a real fillip to our negotiations and we two could come out dancing. Now, how about you join our talks?"

"Great idea, Sonny. Now I'll get online and try to gen myself up before I meet Mr Steinberg."

Kenny Steinberg, as he liked to be called, was not terribly enamoured with the Brits. They were too slow making decisions, and so today he was going to take a hard line – a decision now or he was off to Frankfurt. He waited impatiently in the waiting room for Sonny Rawlings. He was just about to leave when Sonny and some other chap entered the room.

"Good morning, Kenny. Glad you've held on. I've brought my colleague Arthur Spinks to join us because he has access to a near-death person who could get your firm off the ground in Britain, so to speak."

'Now this is more like it,' thought Mr Steinberg.

He stood up quickly to shake Arthur's hand. "Hi. Great to meet you. Now let's get down to business."

Arthur surveyed a young, smartly dressed individual.

"Good morning, Mr Steinberg. My colleague here has put me in the picture to a certain extent; but, as I can sign off any contract between your firm and ours once full agreement has been reached, I shall be grateful to receive detailed information about the cryonics system from you."

"OK, where do you want me to start?"

"The moment of death seems appropriate."

"Right, OK, but actually our team needs to be present before the patient dies; that means of course that the team needs to be informed that demise is imminent. Now, will your National Health Service cooperate, do you think?"

"I'm absolutely sure it will," Arthur reassured him.

"Good. Immediately after death the team will stabilise the corpse's circulation with a heart–lung resuscitator to keep the brain supplied with oxygen, then the body will be packed in ice prior to transit to our facility; it is also injected with a blood-thinning agent. Now, when the body arrives at the facility water will be removed from the corpse."

Arthur was puzzled. "Why is that?"

Mr Steinberg was quite irritated, but answered the question:

"If any internal water in the corpse freezes it forms ice cubes which are not fully joined, and decay can appear in the tissue between them. The last stage is to freeze the corpse to minus 130 degrees Celsius for storage in a state of vitrification."

"How long can the body be kept in that state?"

This time Sonny responded to Arthur because he could see Mr Steinberg's mounting annoyance: "Indefinitely, Arthur, and when medical science has progressed enough to cure whatever killed the person the body can be unfrozen so that remedial surgery or medication or both can be implemented. The first person to be frozen was back in 1967 – that's right, isn't it, Kenny?"

"It sure is and he's still all iced up. Now, guys, I must ask a few questions: first, you know someone close to death – how close?"

Arthur was able to respond: "He's been given less than a year."

"What's wrong with the guy?"

Once again Arthur had the information required: "Melanoma, and it has spread to several organs through his lymphatic system."

"Is this guy willing to undergo cryonics, Arthur?"

"I shall be seeing him at the weekend and I'm very confident he will say yes. He's quite young – early fifties – and he has money. Now I need to know how much expense he and his family will face?"

"OK, fair question. Now, as you know my firm is expanding into Europe; we've chosen to start in the UK because the language is almost the same and there's less religious influence than in some other European countries. Normally we would charge $250,000, but for a first case, and with your firm involved, we can offer a discount down to 200,000."

Sonny turned to Arthur: "Does your relative have that kind of cash, Arthur?"

"Yes. He's a very successful businessman and his firm is on the point of signing a long-term contract with Herculeum."

Arthur could see that both Sonny and Mr Steinberg were impressed.

Mr Steinberg articulated their satisfaction: "Herculeum, you say? Well, that organisation is really big in the States."

"I know that, Kenny."

The American now judged that the Brits were serious, so he

made another offer: "Look, Arthur – I've got a full, illustrated explanation of the process in my attaché case." He leant to his left and pulled out an impressive-looking brochure. "Show this to the guy who is dying – it may help him come to a decision. You must now excuse me because I must contact head office to give them an update."

Both Arthur and Sonny returned to their respective offices feeling distinctly upbeat.

Arthur phoned his wife. "Valerie, I have full details of the cryonics system; it seems really good and could offer both your parents some hope."

"Oh good, Arthur. Mum has phoned me to say Dad is coming out of hospital today; we can talk to him at the weekend. Shall I let Freddie know?"

"If you must."

Valerie was not able to contact her brother – his mobile was switched off and the firm's secretary had no idea where he was. Valerie decided to phone him after work although she knew she would be busy shopping, preparing the evening meal and packing for her and Arthur's trip to Staffordshire.

Arthur arrived home before his wife at the end of the working day. She appeared at the front door forty minutes later.

"Can you help me unloading the car, Arthur, then could you peel the potatoes for me as well? I've got a lot on this evening, you see."

Her husband did not answer verbally, although he followed her out to the car.

"I've got full information on this cryonics system, Val, and the American firm will offer your father a large discount if he decides to sign up with them. Look – after we've eaten, I suggest you read the brochure I've been given; it's very informative."

"I've got a lot to do, Arthur."

"Yes, I recognise that, but any support we can offer both your parents may help them come to terms with a potentially positive outcome to your father's problem."

Valerie made no comment; she was too busy sorting out her purchases.

Margaret picked up her husband from the hospital later that afternoon. She drove; he sat in silence next to her. Margaret was unsure how to engage him conversation. If she tried something trivial she knew, from over twenty-five years' experience, that he could be snappy; on the other hand she didn't want to mention his condition because he might become more morose.

Finally, as they approached the estate: "Does it feel good to be home, Joe?"

"It's better than that bloody hospital."

"Arthur and Val will be with us tomorrow. Arthur's obtained some important information that might give you some real hope, dear."

"I have absolutely no trust in that toffee-nosed twit, Margaret."

His wife was saved from attempting a reply because she was just about to park the car.

Once inside the bungalow Joe went straight to his office.

"I'll call you when dinner is ready, Joe, or, if you like, we could go to The Olive Tree restaurant."

Margaret didn't receive a reply.

At the Spinks' household Valerie managed to contact her brother after she and Arthur had eaten.

"We're coming to the estate tomorrow, Freddie, because Arthur has some positive news about a new system that could give Dad some support."

"Will it extend his life, Val?"

"Well, no, but it could revitalise him in the future."

"Are you sure it is not a scam?"

"Yes, absolutely, so why don't you join us at the estate so you can make your own judgement?" Before Freddie could reply he heard Arthur say something in the background; his sister elucidated for him: "Arthur's just told me that the firm running the system has links to Herculeum, Freddie."

This news was enough to make her brother's mind up. "Right – I'll be there, Val; see you both tomorrow, then."

Later, as they lay in bed, Arthur asked his wife a question: "Did you have chance to read the brochure, dear?"

"Well, I've skimmed it and, as you say, it seems to offer

positive hope. I'll read it thoroughly on our drive up north."

"Good. Now, tomorrow when we meet your dad I'll stay in the background – certainly to start with – because, as you know, he and I do not often see eye to eye on most matters."

Margaret had the most difficult evening of her married life. She had prepared her husband's favourite meal – cottage pie and chips – but he ate it without comment.

Towards the end she did ask him for his assessment: "Have you enjoyed your dinner, Joe?"

His reply was curt: "Yeah, fine. Now I'm going to my study; don't wait up."

She didn't, and when she got upstairs her tears flowed. Finally she fell asleep alone in the bed.

CHAPTER 8

Arthur Spinks' least favourite drive was from London to Staffordshire. He and Valerie had driven in many European countries, the United States, Canada and even Australia, but none had offered the despair of the British motorway system.

"I think I'll take the M1 today, Valerie."

"Do you think that's wise, dear? Remember what happened the last time we went that way. Perhaps we'd better check the road conditions on your iPhone before we set off."

"I am not getting stuck on the wretched M6 near Birmingham, Val; nor am I willing to pay on the toll road."

"Right-ho, dear – as you wish."

Freddie rose late with his latest conquest, Julie.

"I've got to visit my dad today, love, so I can let him know the latest business news."

"How long will you be, Freddie?"

"I'm not totally sure, but if you prepare lunch it'll give an excuse to leave early."

"OK then, just drop me at the supermarket; I can come back here by bus."

Unlike her son, Margaret had wakened early. There was no sign of Joe and his side of the bed had obviously not been slept in. She left the bedroom and went to find him, but he wasn't in the bathroom or the kitchen. For a moment she panicked – perhaps he'd left her! But then she heard a noise from his study.

"Joe, are you in there?"

She received no reply, so she knocked on the door. This time she heard something – a groan possibly. She opened the door and looked in. Joe was sitting with his head on the table; there was an open whisky bottle by his right ear.

"Joe, are you all right?"

Her husband raised his head. "Of course I'm not fucking all right – I'm fucking dying, aren't I?"

Somehow Margaret controlled her need to sob.

"The children are on their way, dear."

Joe stared at her bleary-eyed. "I don't want to see them; I don't want to see anyone; just leave me alone." It was clear that Joe had stayed in his study all night drinking the booze.

"Do you want some breakfast, Joe?"

He didn't answer; he put his head back on the desk and closed his eyes. Tears poured from Margaret's eyes, but she did not sob out loud; quietly she closed the door and went back to the kitchen.

It was time to engage the children again. She phoned Freddie first as he lived quite near.

"Hello, Mum." It was clear from the background noise that her son was in his car.

"Freddie, I need you here. Your dad's in a terrible state."

"I'll be there in twenty minutes, Mum; I'm just going to drop off Julie at the supermarket."

Margaret phoned off and tried her daughter's number.

"Hi, Mum. We're on our way."

"How long before you get here, Valerie?"

This time Arthur spoke: "We're near junction 23A on the M1, Margaret; we should be with you in forty minutes provided the A50 is running smoothly."

"See you soon, then."

Margaret shut her phone down and turned towards the sink; there leaning on the kitchen table was Joe.

"You said something about breakfast."

"Yes, dear, I'll get it now. I've just phoned the kids."

"I heard."

"They'll be here shortly. Arthur has some information for you which sounds promising."

"I don't want to talk to that prig, Margaret."

"Oh, you won't have to – Valerie can do the honours, I'm sure."

"I'll have my breakfast in the study."

"Right you are, Joe."

Freddie arrived first.

"Hi, Mum. How's tricks?"

"Not good, son. Your dad's in a terrible state."

"I've got some good news for him about the contract with Herculeum. Where is he now?"

"In his study; he's been there all night. He's just having his breakfast and he may not want to speak to you." Margaret thought for a second or two before adding, "On the other hand you may be able to take his mind off things."

"OK, Mum. I've brought the draft contract from Herculeum; he needs to sign it and we need someone to witness his signature."

"I'll do that if you like, Freddie."

"Sorry, Mum – we need someone who is not a family member; Val's husband is on his way, isn't he?"

"Yes, but you know what your dad thinks of him."

"Surely Dad can accept him just signing his name. Anyway, I'll go to Dad now."

Margaret was worried, but did not attempt to stop her son. Freddie knocked on the study door and entered.

"Hi there, Dad. I've brought some good news."

His father looked up from his bowl of cereal. "That'll make a change, then, son."

"Yes, I've got the contract drawn up with Herculeum for you to sign."

"I'll be dead before the firm receives any profit."

"Don't be like that, Dad – never say die and all that. Here, have a butcher's at it."

Reluctantly Joe took the document and cast his eye over it quickly."

"What do you reckon, Dad?"

"Seems OK. I'll sign it, but we need an independent witness."

"Arthur is on his way, Dad."

"I want nothing to do with that stuck-up twit."

"He's only got to sign after you; you don't have to speak to him, Dad."

Joe was interrupted before he could say any more because his wife's voice penetrated the study: "Valerie has arrived, Joe." She deliberately didn't mention Arthur. "Freddie, come and meet your sister," she added.

"I'll leave the contract with you, Dad."

"Shut the door as you go out, son, and make sure that stuck-up twit stays away from me."

Margaret ushered her daughter and Arthur into the lounge, where they were joined by Freddie.

"Joe is in a really depressed state; Freddie has just been in to see him. How did he seem to you, son?"

"He showed some interest in the contract I've brought, Mum; he needs to sign it and we need an independent witness to sign as well. Would you do it for us, Arthur?"

"Well, yes, if he agrees, but he doesn't—"

Valerie knew how her husband was likely to finish the statement so she cut in: "We've brought a document too, Mum. It's about a system that can bring the dead back to life sometime in the future. Actually Arthur knows more about it than me."

Arthur interjected at this point: "I'm sure Joe won't listen to me though."

Freddie believed he had an answer to the problem: "You talk to him, Val; call Arthur in if he's interested."

Margaret agreed with her son. "Look, Valerie – come with me now. I'll clear his breakfast things; you can talk to him and show him what you've brought; the men can stay here."

Both men looked relieved.

"Pass me the brochure, Arthur."

Once she had it, Valerie followed her mother to the study. Margaret tapped on the door.

"Valerie is here, Joe; she's got something to show you."

Both women entered. They found Joe staring out of the window across the moor; he didn't turn his head to acknowledge them.

"I'll just clear your breakfast things away, Joe. Valerie is here."

"Hello, Dad. How are—?"

"I'm bloody dying – hasn't anyone told you?"

"Well, yes, but—"

"But bloody what?"

It was time for her to change tack: "Arthur has given me this brochure to show you, Dad."

"Oh yeah – is it about how to join a public school in hell?"

"Look, Dad – he's made a genuine attempt to offer you hope."

"That I'll leave him a few thousand quid in my will?"

Her father's negative attitude overpowered her. Valerie burst into tears and left the room; she dropped the brochure on the table in her grief. She was still sobbing loudly when she rejoined the others.

Arthur was first to react: "What has he done to you, Val?"

His wife couldn't reply through her tears.

"Right, I've had enough – we've come up here through terrible traffic, we've brought some genuine hope and this is what happens. I'm going to have it out with him right now."

"Careful, mate – over my dead body. He's my father, you know."

"I'm aware of that, Freddie, and I know your personal ambitions; has he signed the contract with Herculeum yet? Did you know that firm is associated with The Cryonics Association – a company that offers hope to the dying?" Valerie said this attempting to offer her husband support.

Freddie was nonplussed for once.

Arthur left them and made his way to the study. He didn't knock; he went straight in. Joe was staring out of the window again.

"You have upset my wife – why?"

Joe merely shrugged his shoulders and continued staring into the distance.

"Do you realise, Joe, that you are upsetting the people who are doing their best to support you?"

"Not you though, eh, mate?"

"Look, Joe – I realise that we've never really got on. You don't like me – you think I'm a public-school parasite. Well, I don't like you – to me you're a stuck-in-the-mud yob, but you are not going to upset my wife, who just happens to be your daughter. She came in here earlier to show you information about a process that could offer you a rebirth, and what do you do? Insult her, that's what. I realise you're feeling sorry for yourself, but we've all got to die someday."

Despite their several years of mutual loathing, neither man had uttered such an outburst before.

To Arthur's astonishment Joe turned to face him: "What's this system you're on about, then?"

"The full details are in this brochure which Valerie left on the table for you; briefly it describes a process whereby a newly dead person's body is frozen and preserved intact until such a time when medical science has progressed to the point where the person's illness or illnesses can be cured and the dead person can be brought back to life. The brochure describes the system in much more detail."

"Can it be done on the NHS?"

"Not yet."

"So I'd have to pay."

"Yes, but The Cryonics Association, which is setting up here in Britain, is willing to offer you a special discount."

"How much?"

"Normally, the charge is $250,000 but to you 200,000."

"Bloody 'ell! That's still a packet."

"Well, it's up to you. Personally I don't care what you decide, but, for once, just consider your family; you could offer them hope."

Arthur turned to leave the study; Joe leaned over and picked up the brochure.

"Are you all right, darling?"

Arthur smiled at his wife when he re-entered the lounge. "Well, Val, I think it's true to say that we both made our personal feelings clear, but, as I left, your father was reading the brochure."

Later Joe joined the family for lunch. He ate in silence and so did everyone else because no one knew what to say. Margaret almost asked him what he thought of the brochure, but bit her tongue. Freddie almost mentioned the fact that Herculeum was linked to The Cryonics Association, but he also chickened out. Then he remembered he was supposed to meet Julie, so he left the party. Joe left most of his apple pie and then announced he was returning to his study, much to everyone's relief.

"Perhaps he wants to study the brochure further."

Valerie looked up from her dessert. "Oh, I do hope so, Mum."

Later Joe took his evening meal alone in the study; Margaret carried it through to him on a tray.

"Darling, tonight I've prepared a—" She got no further.

"Is Arthur still 'ere?"

"Yes, Joe. He's just about to start—"

"Tell 'im I want a word."

"Wouldn't you like to eat first?"

"No, I want a word about this cryonics business."

Reluctantly Margaret returned to the dining room.

"Arthur, Joe wants a word with you now."

"I've just started my soup."

"It's about the brochure. Look – I'll keep your food warm for you; Joe's in a bit of a state again."

"OK, then."

Arthur left the room and returned to the study; the door was open. Joe sat facing it; his dinner was on the table before him, untouched.

"You want to talk to me, I believe."

"Yes, about this brochure. I have some questions."

"Fire away – I'll do my best to answer."

"It's about the money. Now, after I'm dead and frozen stiff, where am I kept?"

"The Cryonics Association has a new facility in Heston, near Heathrow Airport. It means expert staff from the United States can access the building more easily."

"OK, so my corpse is stored there, but who is going to keep medical developments under constant review?"

"The association. That's part of what you'd be paying for. Once one of their experts has judged that your cancer can be eradicated, a team will assemble to carry out the new healing procedures. At the moment great strides are being made – for instance, with nanotechnology."

"So they cure me. Then what 'appens?"

"The association informs your family; of course, it can't be exact with the timescale right now because everything depends on the rate of medical progress."

"My wife might be dead then?"

"Yes, and your children and me too possibly, but of course you may have grandchildren or great-grandchildren."

Joe became pensive; Arthur wondered if he should leave, but, as he was about to stand, Joe spoke again: "OK, I'll sign up."

"Good, Joe. I'll text Kenneth Steinberg from the association right now; you'll be their first British client."

Arthur detected what could have been a grin from Joe, and his father-in-law's next remark suggested a lifting of his spirits: "I can sign that contract with Herculeum too and, Arthur, you can witness my signature."

CHAPTER 9

Joe Fenton's health deteriorated very quickly after he signed up for cryonics. Margaret was grateful for all the help she received from a cancer charity as she watched her husband grow weaker almost by the day. Freddie and Valerie worked out a timetable so at least one of them could be present at the estate each weekend; Freddie even dispensed with a girlfriend on his visits.

One dark winter Thursday Joe seemed to reach a crisis point; fortunately Greta Rubina from the charity was in attendance to help Margaret. In the early afternoon Joe fell into a deep sleep and Greta took the opportunity to attempt to prepare Margaret for the next demanding stage in her husband's demise.

"I think, Margaret, that it will be a good idea if we get Joe into a hospice. You see, I doubt if he will live much longer – I have seen several patients in the past with the symptoms he is now showing. In a hospice he will have twenty-four-hour care."

Margaret did not argue, and despite her tears she nodded her agreement.

Two days later Joe entered The Old Oak Hospice. Margaret was present as Joe was wheeled out of the house on a stretcher; she stood by the door to say goodbye. As he passed her on the threshold he looked at her blankly. She tried to say some comforting words, but they wouldn't come out; she rushed back into the lounge in tears, where she steeled herself so that she could accompany Joe to the hospice. Once there, she waited till he was safely installed in his room.

"I must go now, Joe, but I'll be back tomorrow early."

Her words did not register. One of the staff spotted her grief and helped her from the room.

The hospice staff were very helpful. Margaret explained how her husband had signed a contract with The Cryonics Association, and the hospice director agreed to notify both Margaret herself and the association when Joe was approaching his last hours.

She did not have to wait long, because three days later Joe's condition deteriorated further. She rushed to the hospice and arrived at the same time as the cryonics team. A Dr Field rapidly introduced her to his colleagues.

"Can I have one last look at my husband, please?"

"Yes, of course you can, ma'am, while we set up our monitoring equipment."

Margaret entered Joe's room.

The young nurse in attendance whispered to her, "I doubt he will hear you, Mrs Fenton, but you can try."

Joe was lying on his back; his eyes were shut and he was barely breathing. Margaret was totally stuck for words; instead she held out her right hand to touch his cheek. She lurched forward, totally out of control. Fortunately the Nurse caught her arm.

"I think the cryonics people need to come in now, Mrs Fenton." She helped Margaret from the room and took her to the private lounge. "Can you contact anybody, Mrs Fenton?"

"Er, yes, my son. He lives locally."

"Can I call him for you?"

Margaret passed the Nurse her mobile. "Please try his mobile number first."

Freddie did not answer.

"I'll try his business number now, Mrs Fenton."

The firm's secretary answered, but she had no idea where Freddie was.

But then a male voice spoke: "Who is this, please?"

"Nurse Sima at the The Old Oak Hospice; I'm with Mrs Margaret Fenton. Her husband, Joseph, is very ill and Mrs Fenton really does need some family support. I'm having trouble contacting her son and she has told me she also has a daughter who resides in the London area."

There was a pause then a different voice spoke to the Nurse:

"I can help. I'm Rodney Salt – an old friend of the family. Can I speak to Margaret, please?"

Nurse Sima turned to Margaret: "There's a Rodney Salt on the line; he would like to speak to you."

"Yes please, Nurse." Margaret took the mobile. "Rodney, it's Margaret here. Joe's in a very bad way and I can't contact either of my kids."

"No problem, Maggie. I know where the hospice is; I can get there in twenty minutes."

"Thanks, Rodney."

Five minutes after the call the hospice director entered the lounge. His face had a serious expression. He came towards Margaret, who guessed from his body language that Joe had died. Her guess was correct.

"Can I see him, please?"

"I'm afraid not, Mrs Fenton. The cryonics team have started their process – they have to act quickly, you see. They tell me you can visit their facility in Heston next week and view your husband's container."

Margaret slumped back in her chair to await Rodney.

Both children managed to get to the estate the following day, and both were surprised to see Rodney Salt in attendance.

"Rodney has been very good to me; he came to the hospice and he brought me home."

"Did he stay all night, Mum?"

"Yes – we both sat up. I couldn't sleep."

Rodney was sensitive enough to catch the tenor behind Freddie's question.

"Right, folks – now you are all together, I'll leave; I could do with a touch of shut-eye."

"Thank you, Rodney," Margaret called after him. "I'll let you know the funeral arrangements," she added.

Both children were very puzzled by this remark.

Valerie asked the first question: "Can Dad have a funeral, Mum?"

"Yes, of course he can. I have his death certificate."

"But his body is in cold storage, Mum."

"I know that, Freddie, but we need to give him a suitable send-off."

"What kind of service, Mum? Nothing religious surely."

"Valerie, your father was a traditionalist, so, yes, an Anglican Church service, I believe."

"But he didn't go to church, Mum."

"Yes he did, in his boyhood – he was even in the choir, Freddie."

Valerie leapt in to support her brother: "He was asked to leave, Mum, because he couldn't sing in tune – he told me that himself."

Margaret lowered her head and at last both children came to understand that a funeral was very important for their mother.

"Mum, I'll phone the local vicar right now, if you like."

"Please do, Valerie."

The Reverend Phillip Bowden was always extremely busy; he covered five parishes these days and, despite the fact that church congregations were on the way down, there was still a constant demand for his services. Church weddings had remained popular and mourners of the recently deceased often called on his services too. He had noticed, however, that fewer children were being baptised. Valerie Spinks' call was therefore quite a normal event.

"I'm sorry to hear about your father, Mrs Spinks. Now, do you want his body interred or do you prefer a cremation?"

Valerie's reply puzzled him: "My father opted for cryonics, vicar."

"I'm sorry – I don't understand."

"My father chose the process because he hoped to be resurrected sometime in the future."

Valerie expected that her explanation would suffice. It didn't.

"Only the good Lord Jesus was resurrected, Mrs Spinks; the rest of us must await the Day of Judgement."

"My father was a choirboy at an Anglican church, vicar – some years ago, admittedly – and he was confirmed, I believe."

These facts threw a holier light on the situation.

"Look, Mrs Spinks – can I arrange to meet you and other family members? I'm very busy tomorrow, of course, because it's Sunday, but I could meet you later today here at the vicarage."

There was a pause and the vicar heard a conversation in the distance.

"Can we come at two, vicar?"

The Reverend Bowden scanned his laptop. "I can manage three; is that OK?"

Once again he heard other distance voices, but within seconds Valerie confirmed that three o'clock would be fine.

"How many of you will attend, Mrs Spinks?"

"Three or possibly four, vicar. Goodbye for now."

After Valerie put the handset down her mother was quick to thank her.

"Well done, Valerie, I think your resurrection point did the trick. Now, can you all come with me?"

Freddie immediately dropped out. "I'm needed this afternoon, Mum."

"Entering the tender trap again, are you, Freddie?"

Freddie ignored his sister's quip; he bent forward and kissed his mother on the cheek.

"Let me know what you decide, Mum."

Arthur volunteered to drive his wife and mother-in-law to the vicarage; he took the option of entering the vicarage address into his satnav to ensure the party would arrive on time. In the event they were three minutes early, but by the time Arthur had reversed into a parking slot and everyone had left the vehicle they arrived at the front door bang on time. The Reverend Bowden opened up.

"Good afternoon, everyone. I don't think I've had the pleasure before. Now, come into my study – I have enough chairs, I think."

He was one short; Arthur offered to stand, but the vicar insisted he could find an extra one.

While he was searching one out Arthur whispered to his wife, "We need to show him the death certificate."

Fortunately Valerie had brought it in her handbag.

The vicar returned.

"Here we are, everyone. This chair is a bit ancient, like me."

Arthur took the chair from him; the vicar sat behind his desk and faced the threesome. He adopted a more serious demeanour.

"I was very sorry to hear of your recent loss and I must admit I was confused by the term 'cryonics process'; fortunately I have connection to the Internet these days, so I've done some research and I must say I am totally amazed. It seems the Good Lord is offering even more hope for all of us in the future – always provided, of course, that we can afford it."

"So my Joe can have a funeral, then?"

The vicar looked across at Margaret. "Well, no, not a funeral as such, because, you see, there's no body."

Margaret looked as though she was about to burst into tears.

Valerie stepped in to support her: "There is a body, vicar – it's in Heston, near Heathrow Airport."

"Yes, yes, I understand that, but funerals and cremations need a corpse. However, in these rather special circumstances, I can offer a remembrance service."

"In the church?"

"Yes indeed, Mrs Fenton."

Margaret smiled for the first time in days. "Thank you ever so much, vicar."

"I shall need help, of course, in planning the service. I never met Mr Fenton in person, so I have no knowledge of his accomplishments. I can, of course, greet the mourners, but then I would have to rely on facts provided by the family. Perhaps some, or indeed all of you, could play an active part in the service."

The vicar scanned the three faces before him, but there was no immediate reaction from any of them.

Finally Arthur spoke out: "Would it be a good idea, vicar, if we put our heads together and let you know our suggestions?"

"Yes indeed, Mr Spinks, but I must point out that the service should last no longer than thirty minutes. Now, contact me early next week; you can send an email attachment, then I'll write in my part, arrange a date and time and send you a bill. Now I must leave you to prepare my sermon for morning service tomorrow."

Back at the estate Margaret found pens and pencils for all.

"Actually, Margaret, I don't think I'd better be included because I had relatively few dealings with Joe."

Valerie was upset. "Arthur, I know you never really got on with Dad, but surely for this special occasion you could say how Dad welcomed you into the family and how he made such an amusing speech at our wedding."

For once Arthur stepped back. "Well, yes, there is—"

Margaret cut him off: "I know – we could display a picture of

Joe in his prime and play some of Joe's favourite music after the vicar's introduction."

"Oh no, Mum – no one but Dad liked that rock-glam stuff."

"I think you mean glam rock, Margaret."

"Yes, whatever, Arthur." Margaret continued to be creative: "Valerie, you could tell the audience what a great father Joe was and I'll get Freddie to do the same."

Valerie added her own suggestion: "And you, Mum, could tell everyone what a great husband he was – you know, working all those hours, letting you, me and Freddie take holidays without him."

"He was a businessman, Valerie. He was always looking out for us; he bought us this estate; he paid for your college education and he got Freddie an apprenticeship." Margaret's face lit up. "I'll ask Rodney Salt to say a few words about Joe's prowess as a boss."

Valerie wasn't happy. "Mum, we'd have to ensure that Rodney would turn up sober and in suitable attire – and remember, he hardly speaks standard English."

"He's a man of the people, Valerie. He could help bring out Joe's rise from the gutter to prominence. And I've just thought of something else: Rodney knows about personal tragedy. His wife and daughter were killed in a road accident twelve years ago, so he knows about grief from first-hand experience."

"But are you sure he would want to do it, Margaret?"

"Arthur, if I ask him, I'm sure he will."

St Wilfred's Church was looking its best. Margaret had bought bouquets of flowers, which adorned the altar. Arthur had volunteered to hand out the service programme to the mourners as they arrived; the vicar had agreed that one of Joe's favourite tunes would welcome everyone. He wasn't sure that the song 'Rocket Man', sung by someone called Elton John, was totally suitable, but of course this was not a funeral but a remembrance. Now, as he stood by the altar, he waited till the final plaintive notes faded away. He scanned the congregation and estimated that about thirty people were present. He took a deep gulp of breath.

"Good afternoon, everybody. We are here today to remember

and celebrate the life of Joseph Fenton. As I am sure you are all aware, Joseph has chosen to have his body preserved so that, sometime in the future, he can be resurrected; now, as a Christian, I know that the Lord Jesus Christ rose from the dead and therefore I can conduct this service. I never knew Joseph myself, so I am going to call on members of his family and friends to share their recollections with us all. First, Joseph's wife will speak to us."

Margaret took a deep breath; Valerie held her hand as she stood up ready to mount the altar steps.

"Come with me, Val, please," Margaret whispered.

Together the two women walked to their positions; both turned to face the congregation. Margaret cleared her throat.

"Thank you all for attending; you are a great comfort to me personally and I am sure to Joe's children as well. One of the first things that attracted me to Joe was his handsome looks; I eventually became his secretary and I came to love his sense of humour, which, allied to his business acumen and hard work, ensured his success both as a boss and later as a husband and father. He was born into poverty – his parents divorced and he lived in a poor suburb for many years – but he thrived at school and he was determined to gain skills in the building trade. We got married when he was twenty-one and I was nineteen, and through hard work and sensitivity we formed a devoted team. We were blessed with two children, and Joe's high expectations for them means that they too are now leading successful working lives."

Margaret paused for breath.

Valerie took up the panegyric: "I agree with all that Mum has just said, but I must add that Mum here played a more than equal part in my and Freddie's upbringing, and her devotion to my father has been undying, especially in the days when his life was ebbing away."

Margaret could contain herself no longer – her tears flowed. She gripped her daughter's arm and they returned to their pew.

The Reverend Bowden glanced down at his programme. "Now, ladies and gentlemen, Frederick, Joe's son, wants to say a few words."

This was the moment Freddie had been dreading. He had no experience of addressing an audience; hitherto all his adult communication had been with workmates, family and numerous girlfriends. He had only very reluctantly agreed to his mother's request to avoid upsetting her. Julie, his latest lover, had been very helpful though.

"Tell them something you remember from your childhood, Freddie – something amusing."

"But what?" he had asked.

"I don't know, do I? What about football? You told me he used to take you to watch Stoke City."

Freddie had given the matter much thought and had even written out a short speech. Now as he faced the congregation he pulled it from his pocket.

"My dad loved football and I always remember the times he took me to watch his favourite team. He used to join in the chit-chat with other spectators and he was very knowledgeable and funny. I remember one match when Stoke had signed a new central defender; I asked him at half-time if he thought the new guy was any good. He looked down at me and said, 'Well, Freddie, he's not bad, but he needs to catch a bus when he turns round.' Everyone round us laughed out loud." To his surprise Freddie detected some stifled merriment in the congregation, so he went on: "I owe a lot to my dad. He taught me all I know, and before he died he was able to sign a contract with a major company. This means that our firm, Fenton & Son, will be profitable for many, many years to come. Thank you, Dad."

As he went to sit down he became aware of a very different reaction: many in the congregation were wiping their eyes.

As he passed his mother she whispered to him, "Well done, Freddie."

The Reverend Bowden took the initiative again: "This service has been a revelation for me because I am now aware that a former choirboy rose from the lower orders to become a person of substance both in business and also in family life. I now invite Joe Fenton's oldest friend to address us before my final prayer."

Margaret clutched her daughter's arm again. Rodney Salt, like Freddie before him, did not consider himself to be an orator; he also had reluctantly agreed to Margaret's request to help her through her sorrow. Today he hadn't touched a drop of alcohol for at least six hours and he had had a haircut – his first for two months. His suit was obviously old and, as he passed Margaret and Valerie, the smell of mothballs was very noticeable. His hands were shaking as he fished out his speech from his jacket pocket.

"Hello, everyone. My name is Rodney Salt and I've known Joe since we were lads. We were at school together, and that's where Joe first helped me. He was bright; I wasn't. He looked out for me always. We left school at the same time and we both became apprenticed to the same firm. When Joe set up his own business he immediately offered me a job. That was over thirty years ago. He was a good boss because he knew what it was like for lads with backgrounds like ours. He was on our wavelength. His most important support for me came when my wife and daughter were killed in a road accident twelve years ago. He would sit with me and listen; he would check that, outside the working day, I wasn't alone for too long; and he paid for both funerals. I can never forget him and I ask you all here now to support Margaret at this sad time in the same way that Joe cared for me."

Rodney lowered his head, wiped his nose with the back of his left hand and returned to his seat.

The service entered its final phase: the Reverend Bowden offered a final prayer. "Dear Lord, we here today commend our dear family member and friend to eternal life in heaven to be by Your side. Amen." He wasn't finished, however, because, once everyone had raised their eyes, he continued: "As I'm sure you all know, Joseph has engaged the latest scientific technology to conserve his body so that, if and when progress permits, he can be resurrected; this may not happen in our lifetimes or indeed ever. Personally I hope that such a good person, like Mr Fenton, can indeed be brought back to life, and it is with that hope I now play a final hymn much beloved by soccer fans. Please stand for 'Abide with Me'."

Later the family, Rodney Salt and a few other workmates went to Joe's favourite pub, where the landlord had prepared his usual meal of fish and chips. Everyone except Arthur tucked in with gusto. As was normal, Arthur felt somewhat excluded.

PART TWO: THE RESURRECTION

CHAPTER 1

Yellow, all-encompassing yellow, then a noise – a buzzing sound – then a shape came into view which materialised into a face.

"Mr Fenton, can you hear me?"

Joe couldn't answer; his senses were overwhelmed. He closed his eyes.

He heard a different voice: "Has he passed out or has he died again?"

The first voice responded: "Remember he has been dead for forty-one years; this situation must be completely overpowering. We must wait till he feels he can communicate with us."

Hours later Joe's thirst became pressing; his mouth was totally dry. He opened and closed it several times, attempting to ask for water.

"Bella, he's trying to speak." The first face appeared to Joe again. "Can I get you something, Mr Fenton?"

"Water."

"He needs water, Carlos."

Joe felt a hand behind his neck and an upward pressure.

"Sip this slowly, Mr Fenton."

A cool flow slipped through Joe's mouth; when it reached the back of his throat he spluttered.

"Careful, Mr Fenton – take it nice and slowly." A male face came into vision. "I'll wipe your mouth, Mr Fenton."

Now the female face reappeared.

"I'm Bella, Mr Fenton."

The information meant nothing to Joe.

"Where am I? What's happening to me?"

"You have been brought back to life, Mr Fenton. When you died forty years ago your body was preserved by the cryonics process until medical science could rectify your cancer. I'm pleased to tell you that progress in surgical techniques has allowed Vistula surgeons to be able to revive you intact; you are alive once more."

Joe's confusion still raged.

The one called Bella offered more clarification: "I feel sure that you will soon recall that forty years ago you died, but before you passed away you signed up for cryonics so that your corpse would be preserved until such time as you could be resurrected; that time is now, Mr Fenton."

Joe attempted to sit up; the one called Carlos helped him. From his upright position Joe could see he was in some kind of operating theatre with two doctors or nurses; slowly his long-term memory clicked into gear. Yes, cryonics – he remembered something about cryonics. A brochure – he remembered reading a brochure. Bella noticed his change of attitude.

"Are you beginning to remember, Mr Fenton?"

Joe cleared his throat. "Yes, indeed. My wife and children – where are they, please?"

"I have made contact with your son. He will come to see you quite soon."

"And my wife?"

Bella knew this moment would come because Joe Fenton was the first person in the cryonics system who had ever been brought back to life. Bella had been present when three other corpses had remained dead despite the best efforts of skilful surgeons and other AI robots.

She answered Joe's question as diplomatically as possible: "Your son, Frederick, will fill you in with all facts about your family, Mr Fenton." She then moved on quickly: "Now, over the next few days we here at the Vistula Centre will check out all your body's systems – circulation, breathing, digestion and movement – so that hopefully you can return to normal life. How does that sound?"

Joe didn't answer verbally, he merely smiled.

"Right then, Mr Fenton – Carlos and I will leave you to get some rest."

Joe lay back, but the last thing he could do was rest; his memory went almost berserk.

He was back in Chell, a working-class district of Stoke-on-Trent. He remembered the tatty kitchen and how one day he had found his mother crying with her head down on the table. He had started crying as well. His mother had picked him up and cuddled him, but both of them had continued to shed tears. He remembered the frequent rows between his parents – often he heard the altercations from his pokey bedroom; sometimes he covered his ears with the pillow.

The family troubles had come to a climax when he was about five years old. He was wakened by his mother's screaming; the man he believed to be his father was ranting wildly. He had heard a door slam. He had jumped out of bed worried that his mother had left. She hadn't – he had found her on her knees in the kitchen with blood streaming from her nose. He had never seen the man he called Father from that day on.

Joe tried to dismiss such troubled memories. After all, he was alive again and a new reality beckoned. He tried to sleep, and this time a happier memory came to the fore. It was Christmas; he was eight; he had sneaked downstairs very early; he had hung his stocking in the lounge. When he entered he had a great shock: propped up by the Christmas tree was a new bike. He couldn't believe it – surely the bike wasn't his. As he went to touch it his mother and Uncle Ted entered the lounge.

"Happy Christmas, Joe."

"Is this mine, Mum?"

"Yes, of course it is, Joe. You must thank your uncle – he asked Santa to bring it for you."

"Thanks, Uncle Ted," he had said.

"Santa had a hell of a job getting it down the chimney, Joe."

Joe now smiled again as he remembered his uncle's joke, and at last he went to sleep.

He had a sequence of dreams. In one, Margaret appeared before him; she was young and smiling. She opened her mouth as though to speak, but no words came out. Then she vanished.

Later he dreamt of his mother when she was working as a housekeeper in a rectory. She and Joe lived in a small flat on the top floor; Joe remembered how he had hated his life there.

The rector was a strange individual who had encouraged Joe to join the church choir; his mother agreed with the clergyman and insisted he took part. There were only three other choirboys. Each Thursday evening they had to practise under the rector's sole guidance. Joe soon came to understand that religious music was not the major thing on the rector's mind: he would insist each boy stand upright and, to force them into the correct posture, he would press each boy's buttocks; once he even slipped his hand into Joe's trousers. Joe deliberately sang as badly as possible; the rector offered to give him extra tuition, but, fortunately for Joe, Thursday became his soccer-practice evening. The rector directed his efforts elsewhere after dismissing Joe from the choir. With this recollection Joe finally fell into a dreamless sleep.

The next day Joe awoke early. Once again memories came to dominate his thoughts. He now remembered that, as soon as he could, he had left the rectory and, together with his friend Rodney, he had found a small flat in town where he had stayed until he had married Margaret. Where was Margaret now? he wondered. Why had she not come to see him?

"Your breakfast is here, Mr Fenton." Carlos's strange mechanical voice interrupted his memories. He was holding a plate upon which there was an oddly shaped biscuit.

"What is this, please?" Joe asked.

"It is a Vistula cracker, which contains all the nourishment required to sustain a human person like you."

"Can I have a coffee, please?"

"No, Mr Fenton, coffee is not available, but I will bring you a beaker of Vistula water, which is also highly nutritious."

Joe was not happy, but he was hungry so he ate the tasteless biscuit and then drank the equally bland liquid. When he had finished Bella entered the room.

"Today, Mr Fenton, we will help you to walk again. The cryonics procedure should have preserved your muscle strength as it was, but we will check it with you and, if all is well, I will contact your son, who can come to take you home."

Joe's mood lifted because he was keen to return to the estate and greet the family.

It took Joe some time to walk unaided. First he had trouble

with his balance, then with coordinating his steps, but finally, after what seemed like several hours, he managed to walk ten or so metres without help.

"Right, Mr Fenton, you are mobile enough to join your son. I'll contact him now. He should be here within a quarter of an hour. Sit on that chair; do not attempt to move before your son arrives. Carlos and I must leave you now."

Joe attempted to thank them, but they both turned away from him and left the room. He sat on the chair as directed and found that he couldn't stand up even if he had wanted to; the chair's arms pressed into him, forming a firm but painless trap.

A short time later Joe heard a swishing sound to his right. He turned his head just as a person entered the room. Surely this couldn't be Freddie. The person now standing before him was certainly male, but he was skinny, bald and aged. There was one thing though that gave Joe some hope: the man now standing before him was wearing a grey overall, the same as Carlos and Bella.

"Hello, Dad. It's me."

Joe examined the person again; his appearance was puzzling, but the voice was just as Joe remembered it.

"Is that really you, Freddie?"

"Yes, Dad, it is. Now let me help you up, because we must leave here pronto."

"I'm stuck in this bloody chair, son."

"I'll sort it, Dad."

Freddie pulled back the sleeve on his right arm; he was wearing some kind of wristwatch. He took a short, pen-like stick from his breast pocket and pressed the watch thing; Joe felt the chair's arms lose their pressure.

"Come on, Dad – we've got to go."

"Where—?"

Freddie interrupted his father: "I'll tell you everything when we get home."

He held the door open and Joe shuffled through to the outside world. His jaw dropped open – before him was the strangest vehicle he had ever seen. It was a flat-bottomed blob with no windows. Freddie pushed past him and activated the watch thing again. Joe watched in wonder as a panel on the side of the vehicle slid open.

"Get in, Dad, please."

"Is this thing yours, son?"

"No questions yet, Dad; just get in and take a seat."

Joe followed his son's order; immediately he noticed there was no driver present. He turned to Freddie, but before he could utter a word his son put an index figure to his lips. The message was obvious: no talking. The next sensation amazed Joe again. He felt the vehicle lift slightly, then a gentle fizzing sound became apparent as the thing moved. Freddie touched his arm and pointed to a screen which Joe had not noticed up to this point. Clearly the picture showed the world outside as it flashed by. Joe was amazed by the number of young fir trees; he saw no dwellings or people, just trees and other plants. He turned to question his son, but once again Freddie indicated that, for the moment at least, all verbal communication was off limits.

After ten minutes or so Joe became aware that the vehicle was slowing down; when it came to a stop, it dropped down gently and the panel opened silently. Freddie touched Joe's arm again and gestured that they should get out. Once outside, Joe's confusion increased. There was no sign of his estate; he found himself staring at a dome-shaped building made of some unknown opaque material.

"This is my home, Dad. Follow me in and I'll show you round."

Inside, the main room was dominated by a large flat screen. 'Well,' Joe thought, 'at least there's television.' There was a low sofa and a couple of easy chairs. Three doors led off the room.

Freddie pointed to one of them. "Come with me, Dad."

He pushed the door open and once again Joe recognised something normal – a bathroom.

"You sit on the toilet, Dad; I'll prop myself by the sink."

Freddie turned the cold tap on.

"What the heck are you doing, son?"

Freddie smiled. "We can't be overheard in here with the water running, Dad."

"Please, Freddie, tell me what this is all about."

"You died just over forty years ago, Dad, and in the intervening time everything has changed dramatically. I'll try to explain, but it will be best if you ask the questions."

Joe had so many questions that he had great difficulty prioritising them. Finally, after a minute or so, he decided the family should come first.

"Where's your mother, Freddie? I thought she would be here to meet me."

Joe couldn't help noticing his son's mournful expression as he replied, "I'm afraid you can't see her, Dad."

"Why not?"

"She passed away twelve years ago."

"Do you mean she's dead?"

"Remember, Dad, that you've been dead over forty years. If you had lived you would now be ninety-one; Mum died when she was nearly eighty. She outlived her husband by six years."

"What the hell are you talking about, son? I'm her husband. I accept that she's died and that she outlived me by twenty-eight years, so what's all this nonsense about six years?"

Freddie had been dreading this moment. He lowered his head before explaining.

"After you died, Dad, Mum married again."

"She did what?"

Joe's raised voice increased Freddie's obvious distress, but he had no option but to answer: "Mum was in a very sorry state after your death; she needed support, but, unfortunately, both Valerie and I had to work so she turned to the one person she knew who had time on his hands."

"Who was that, then?"

"Your old pal, Rodney Salt."

Joe took a moment or two for this fact to sink in.

"Are you telling me that she married Rod?"

"Yes, Dad."

"Well, the disgusting bastard! I take it he's dead or else I'd have his cock for breakfast; he's not been frozen, has he?"

"No, Dad, he was cremated."

"That's good because if he was frozen I'd soon warm the dirty bugger up." Another urgent subject came into Joe's consciousness: "What about the estate, Freddie? What's happened to the bloody estate?"

"Mum sold it after Rod's death; actually it's a good job she did because, shortly after the sale, the whole of the Staffordshire moors caught fire. The new owners were burnt to death."

"So where did she live?"

"With me and Julie."

"Who the hell is Julie?"

"You met her years ago, Dad – she was my girlfriend then, but we got married."

Joe combed his memory. Finally he remembered a barbecue where a young lass took over the cooking.

"Why did Margaret live with you, then?"

"Well, she had problems with her nerves, but we were quite happy because she was pretty rich after the sale of the estate."

"Did she leave you the lot, son?"

"No – like you, she paid for cryonics. I'm not exactly sure where her body is now – it might be stored at Heston, like you were. She had breast cancer, and I believe that nowadays most forms of the condition can be cured, so you may meet her again soon."

The look on his father's face told Freddie that any meeting might be problematic, so he attempted to change the subject.

"Valerie is still going strong, Dad."

The ruse worked.

"Is she still married to that stuck-up prat?"

"Oh, you mean Arthur. Yes, he's still around. I'll try to arrange a meeting if you like. They have a child – well, actually now she's a mature adult. Her name's Melissa."

Before Joe could respond he and Freddie heard the main door open.

"That'll be Julie, Dad."

Freddie pulled himself upright and left the bathroom; Joe followed him after turning off the tap.

He found himself gazing at an elderly woman wearing the same colour overall as Freddie, who now greeted her: "Oh, hi, Julie. Dad's here. I told you Vistula Health had arranged for him to stay with us."

Julie turned to Joe, but before she could utter a word the screen on the wall burst into life.

The picture showed flames engulfing a hillside, and then a

monotone voice spoke: "Eat now. Lights out one hour."

"Who the hell was that?"

"That was Vistula Domicile, Dad. It runs the food supply and the electricity. We can chat now because it's close to shutdown time."

"Are you telling me, Freddie, that you don't even control your diet, your viewing or your power supply?"

"Yes, Dad. I told you earlier that many things have changed since your death; now we need to eat immediately before the light goes out."

Julie left them and went through one of the other doors.

"Julie will bring the nosh, Dad; we can sit on the sofa to eat it. It may not look like much, but it will have the full range of nourishment. Obesity is a thing of the past."

"Have you got some wine, Freddie?"

"No, Dad. No one sells alcohol any more, but we can all have a glass of Vistula fruit cocktail – it's very nice."

Joe was still processing this information when Julie returned carrying a large cardboard plate on which there were three tiered biscuits and three small transparent beakers, each containing the same pale grey liquid.

"Dinner is served, folks," Julie announced.

"How did you get on today, Julie?" Joe's son asked this after finishing his biscuit.

"It was dreadful, Freddie. We had to pick corn on the cob for five hours without a break, but I've earned us 300 points."

Freddie noticed his father's totally confused expression; he attempted to give him some clarity: "This is one of the really big changes, Dad, since you left us – there's no money any more."

"How the hell—?"

Freddie interrupted: "We live by points, Dad. Every day, as long as we don't step out of line, Vistula Finance awards us 200 points each; now today, as you've just heard, Julie has been awarded 300 extra."

Joe was still confused. "What do you use these bloody points for, then?"

This time Julie answered: "Everything, Joe – food, shelter, transport, health . . . You name it, points cover it."

"So did you choose to work, then, Julie?"

"In a way, yes. I got a message on my wrist monitor" – here she held up her arm to show Joe the device – "telling me I would be picked up at 1100 hours for work."

"And if you didn't show, what then, Julie?"

"I would have been debited 100 points."

Freddie took up the explanation: "Anyone who falls to zero points is picked up by the SS."

At last Joe felt he had something relevant for the conversation.

"Don't be bloody stupid, son – the SS was present in Nazi Germany, and that must be well over 100 years ago. I forget what the letters stood for; it was something like Shits Staffeln."

"Right – well, now, Dad, the letters stand for Swoop Squad and anyone falling to zero is removed and never seen again."

"Surely, son, they do a runner before they're picked up."

"No point, Dad. The SS can enter every house and they can track everyone's movements."

Joe was really startled. "How?"

"I don't know if you noticed, Dad, but when I brought you here to the house I didn't use a key to get in; I just held my right wrist monitor up to the door handle, which opened the door immediately. This means, of course, that the SS can enter at any time, and if people try to escape they can be found wherever they attempt to hide."

At this point Julie pointed upwards to the ceiling. "See that grill up there, Joe? Well, Vistula Domicile can listen to every conversation and it can make poisonous gas enter the property too."

"That's why I took you to the bathroom, Dad – there's no grill in that room."

Joe was speechless.

Freddie had more to add: "Tomorrow I have to register you with Vistula Domicile. It already knows you are here because Vistula Health will have sent it a message, but you need a code number and two wrist monitors, like me and Julie have, so you too can earn points."

Joe was about to complain, but the dim lighting suddenly flickered.

The screen lit up again and the voice made an announcement: "Five minutes to lights out."

"You're in the spare room, Dad – it's the door on your right. By the way, you must change out of your old clothes and wear the Vistula uniform like everybody else."

"What happens to my clothes, then, son?"

"I'm not sure, but probably the Swoop Squad will collect them, so just leave them in the bedroom."

Joe had never attempted to sleep in a totally darkened room before in his life; he lay awake still fully clothed because he couldn't find a uniform anywhere. What on Earth was going on? he wondered. Never in his wildest thoughts had he imagined a world like this. Why had this Vistula lot brought him back to life? Did he want to live like this? The awkward side of his personality finally took over – he must do something. What exactly, he wasn't sure, but something definitely. In this defiant mood he finally fell asleep.

CHAPTER 2

What the hell was making that noise? Joe awoke with a start – it sounded like a bugle call. The ceiling light came on; the bedroom door opened and Freddie entered.

"Time to get up, Dad – the drone will be here shortly."

"What's going on now, son?"

"As I've just told you, Dad, it's wake-up time. Here's your uniform – a drone delivered it very early today. Julie's already having a shower; you can follow her and I'll collect the food from the next drone."

Joe could still not make sense of what was happening, but he had no opportunity to seek enlightenment because Freddie left the room.

Joe straightened his new apparel as best he could, then he heard Julie call to him: "Shower's free, Joe."

At last something Joe could enjoy – a warm shower. He found a soap dispenser and covered himself before directing the nozzle at his body. He doused his head first, then his chest, but then, suddenly and without any warning, the water shut off, leaving his lower body all soaped up.

"Julie how the hell do I start the shower again?"

Her reply annoyed him: "You can't, Joe – you've had your time."

Reluctantly he stepped out and dried himself as best he could. He was rubbing his right foot when he heard a swishing sound somewhere overhead.

"What's that noise, Julie?"

"It's OK, Joe; it's only the drone delivering the day's food and drink."

For breakfast Joe had to eat another of those biscuit things; surprisingly, this one had a slight bacon-and-egg tang. When he had finished it Julie handed him a cardboard cup that was obviously waterproof because it had liquid inside it which had a slight coffee flavour. Joe sat back unclear what should happen next; Freddie knew what to do.

"Right, Dad – I must contact Vistula Domicile right away and register you so you can receive wrist monitors and earn points to pay for your upkeep."

Joe watched keenly as his son turned his left wrist monitor upwards before he poked the dial with his index finger.

"What are you doing now, son?"

"First, Dad, I have to log on using my personal code; this property is located in Global 069, so I enter the three digits then I leave a space before I enter my personal number."

Joe continued to observe.

Suddenly, without warning, the device on his right wrist burst into life. Freddie lifted it to his lips.

"Domicile, please."

After a short pause, Joe heard a tinny-sounding voice: "Reason?"

"New person's registration."

"Enter name and sex."

Joe could only watch as Freddie entered the required details.

There was another short pause before the tin-voiced person spoke again: "Person not recognised. Registration denied."

"Oh, bollocks!"

"What's up, Freddie?"

"There's obviously been a glitch, Dad; Vistula Health has either sent the wrong details or, because your situation is unique, the system cannot cope."

Julie gasped. "Without official registration, Joe, you'll receive no food."

"What the hell do I do then?"

Joe received no immediate answer because both Freddie and Julie were deep in thought.

After perhaps two minutes Julie spoke up: "What we need is someone more knowledgeable and up to date than us; therefore we must arrange a meeting with Valerie and Arthur."

Freddie was not convinced. "Hang on a bit, Julie – Valerie is less savvy than we are and Arthur is not the brain he once was."

"I know that, dear, but there's their daughter, Melissa. She's really bright and with it – I'm sure she could help."

Joe brightened up. "Good idea, Julie. Just give her a call or send a text."

"Sorry, Dad, but it's not that easy; I'll have to contact her through Vistula Communication."

Julie offered to help: "I'll try for you, dear. You see, Joe, Freddie is allowed to visit a close relative twice a year; he could take you with him and, because you are not yet completely on Vistula's radar, they won't be able to prevent you going as well. It's worth a try, surely."

Both males agreed with the suggestion.

"You've never met your granddaughter, have you, Dad?"

"No, son, I haven't. How old is she, by the way?"

Julie knew. "She's forty-eight."

"How do we get to her, Julie?"

"If Vistula agrees, they'll send a mobile blob like the one that brought us here yesterday."

Julie left the men and went to the main bedroom; she returned after ten minutes.

"Right, gents, both Vistula and Melissa have agreed and the transport will be here at 1500 hours. Freddie, you can stay for two hours, but your dad can remain for as long as he likes, presumably because he's off the system. Vistula will charge me and Freddie twenty-five points each though."

All three now relaxed, but their leisure was interrupted by the screen, which burst into life again.

"Julie Fenton required for work. Meet transport in five minutes."

"Well, there you go, Julie; you'll earn us some more points."

Julie was obviously not amused by her husband's remark.

When Julie had left the house Joe posed more questions to his son. "This Vistula thing, Freddie – what the hell is it?"

"It's the system that runs everything these days, Dad."

"But how the hell did it take over?"

"I'm not totally sure, but, I tell you what, Melissa may know so you can ask her later today. She's very bright and she retains information well."

Unfortunately for Freddie, Joe had other pressing concerns.

"What happened to our firm, Freddie – you know, Fenton & Son."

This was another topic Freddie had been dreading, but he knew he must answer: "It went bust, Dad."

"How the hell did that happen?"

"If you remember, just before you died we signed a contract with Herculeum, that global firm. I prepared our firm for the contracted work – I bought all the stuff required – but Herculeum got caught up in a massive business turndown. You may remember the big problem in 2008; well, the big bust in 2027 was far worse. Everything went haywire across the whole world. It's now referred to as the Great Upheaval. That was when Vistula came to the fore. Now, I don't know the full details, but Arthur's firm became very involved and I'm sure he'll be able to give you much more detail than I can – that's assuming he hasn't lost all his marbles after his stroke, of course."

"Did you say Arthur's had a stroke?"

"Yes, Dad, about two years ago, I think. He's made a recovery of sorts and we'll find out later today what kind of shape he's in."

Two blobs arrived about five minutes later. Julie had to embark on the larger of the two. As the side panel opened Joe noticed about ten other passengers all presumably on the same work detail; they were all sitting with their heads facing down and all were uncommunicative.

"Come on, Dad – we need to enter our transport."

Julie had found Freddie's spare overall before she left the house; Joe put it in a paper bag. He guessed it wasn't going to be a perfect fit – he was sure that it would be too tight around the waist – but at least it would prevent him from standing out from everyone else while his other uniform was being cleaned. Once in the blob, the door panel closed; the machine lifted and they were off. Freddie nudged his father and pointed to the screen before once more raising his right index finger to his lips.

The pictures that came to Joe's eyes amazed him – there was devastation everywhere. Not one brick or concrete building was intact, so every town or village the blob passed appeared completely deserted. There were, however, some properties, similar to his son's. All were dome-shaped and made from the same opaque plastic material. Joe was also surprised by the number of trees; most were evergreen and most were young, and around their roots there appeared to be a network of fine wires. Several times Joe turned to Freddie, but each time his son refused to make eye contact, so Joe's many questions went unasked – for the time being, at least.

This journey was far longer than the one Joe had experienced before and the blob was travelling far more quickly; the images on the screen flashed by.

Suddenly the screen went blank and the blob came to a stop, then, from somewhere in the vehicle, a metallic voice piped up: "Two hours, Frederick."

Then the panel opened and the two Fentons exited. Joe found himself staring at another dome-shaped building, but this one was certainly larger than Freddie's. Freddie tapped something into his right wrist monitor and within seconds a door in the building slid open.

"Come on, Dad – we can enter."

Inside the light was dim, but an inner door opened and an elderly woman appeared; she was wizened and lined and had a walking stick in her right hand.

Freddie addressed her: "Hi, Valerie. I've brought Dad as promised."

Surely this could not be his daughter, Joe thought, but when she spoke the voice was as he remembered it: "Dad, this is amazing. How are you?"

"Well, OK, I guess" was all Joe could manage in reply.

"Come and meet Arthur, both of you; he's sitting in his room. He's not very active these days, you see."

"You go first, Dad."

Joe complied with his son's request and entered what was obviously a bedroom. There was a single bed and one armchair, sitting on which was a crumpled figure who didn't look up.

Valerie called over Joe's shoulder: "My father's here to see you, darling."

With an obvious strain, Darling raised his head and looked at Joe, but he showed no sign of recognising the guest.

"We'll try again later, Dad; come and sit in the lounge with me and Freddie."

Her brother rejected his sister's suggestion. "Actually, Val, if you don't mind, I'll return to the blob so it can take me home; Julie and I won't lose as many points if I go now, and I'm sure you and Dad will have lots to discuss. Where's Melissa, by the way?"

"Oh, she's had to work today, but she should be back any minute."

"Right – I'll get off, then, Dad; Val can let me know any developments. I'll see you later."

With this Freddie left the building.

"Can I get you a drink, Dad?"

"Oh, yes please, Val – a coffee would be great."

"Sorry – there's no coffee any more; the best I can manage is Vistula water."

Joe nodded his agreement.

Valerie left him, so he gazed around the room. It was much more spacious than his son's main living area. Joe reckoned there was seating for six adults; once again there was a large screen on one wall. Joe looked up at the curved ceiling – there, directly above him, was the same-sized grill as in Freddie's property.

"Here's your drink, Dad." Valerie handed him a cardboard cup.

Joe took a sip and to his delight found that the liquid had the taste of dry white wine. Valerie sat beside him. Joe pointed up at the grill and raised his eyebrows.

"It's OK, Dad – we're not being overheard."

"How do you know that, Val?"

"Because there is no small red glow from the centre; Arthur worked that out before he became ill, but we must keep our eye on the grill while we chat. Now, how are you getting on in your second life?"

"I can't get my head round the changes, Val. I mean it's only forty years since my death – what the hell has happened?"

"No one totally understands what's occurred, Dad. I can perhaps describe for you the sequence of events that led up to the present situation, but Melissa will be able to fill in more detail, I'm sure."

"OK, Val, tell me what you know."

"I wonder, Dad, if you remember the concerns about global warming before you died?"

"It was a load of nonsense, Val. I agreed with that American president – I forget his name."

"He was wrong, Dad, and so were you, because shortly after your remembrance service the world's weather went haywire. There were massive storms and earthquakes; polar ice melted quickly, which caused extensive flooding in some areas, like here in Global 069."

"Look, Val – if you mean Britain just say it."

"Sorry, Dad. There's no Great Britain any more, or any other nations for that matter; we are now in Global 069 and this property is located in what used to be East Anglia. The region almost disappeared in the storms, as did Holland. In other parts of the world the land rose and huge fires broke out. Global 088 became uninhabitable."

"Where the hell is Global 088?"

"Australia. It became a huge desert and millions of people had to attempt to emigrate; thousands upon thousands were drowned in the Pacific Ocean. Emigration became a major problem and countries less affected, like Global 003 – that was Russia, by the way – tried to stop any influx. The United Nations Organisation attempted to negotiate an agreed system, but it failed; this led to war between the bigger countries. There was chaos made much worse by an outbreak of septic influenza, which killed millions including both Arthur's parents. For a time it seemed the human race was doomed, but, of course, in such a situation there can be a few winners. Some massive technology companies saw opportunities to make sustained profits. Arthur's firm was one of them. Now, I know you've heard about Vistula."

"I certainly have, Val – it seems to dominate everything."

"I does indeed, Dad. It started as a small, high-tech firm, but its rapid development of algorithms, artificial intelligence and robotics meant that other huge organisations came to rely on it because Vistula's systems offered ways to reduce the chaos and thus preserve any profits from what life remained on the planet. Within two decades Vistula had absorbed all the competition and its power could not be challenged. This was the main result of the Great Upheaval. When you meet Melissa she can add more detail, I'm sure."

Once again Joe was struggling to comprehend what he had been told.

The big picture was beyond him, so he reverted to the more mundane: "So how long have you lived here, Val?"

"It must be twenty-five years or so. Our place in Harrow was bombed to bits in World War Three. Fortunately Arthur and I were on holiday in northern Scotland at the time, and when peace arrived Arthur was offered this property."

"Why?"

"Well, as I've already told you, he was well in with Vistula. You may not like this house, Dad, but it's top-drawer these days."

Joe had already recognised that his daughter's residence had more space and comfort than his son's had.

"What's wrong with Arthur, Val?"

"He had a stroke two years ago."

"Can the doctors cure him?"

"There are no doctors in the sense you would understand. When he collapsed I contacted Vistula Health on my wrist monitor; I described his symptoms and almost immediately it sent a blob with two robots and medication. They saved his life and now they check on him regularly. Normally a person in Arthur's condition would be discarded, but I guess his previous work with Vistula means that he has some privileged status. I haven't a clue how long Vistula will continue its involvement – in fact, every day I'm expecting a visit from the Swoop Squad."

At this point in the conversation Valerie became very upset; Joe kept quiet and concentrated on what remained of his drink.

CHAPTER 3

Melissa entered the property when twilight was developing. Both Joe and Valerie heard the main door open.

"We're in here, darling," Valerie called out.

"I'll just say hello to Dad first, Mum."

"Melissa is very close to her father, Dad; she was devastated when he had his stroke."

Joe was about to ask if his granddaughter was married, but stopped when she entered the room. He found himself looking at a tall, slim, mature woman whose stature and demeanour certainly favoured her father.

"I have a big surprise for you, Mel." Here Valerie pointed towards Joe. "This is your grandfather."

Melissa stared at Joe for a moment before reacting vocally: "Impossible, Mum – my granddad has been dead for years. This is an imposter, probably sent by the SS."

"No, no, darling, this really is him; tell her, Dad, please."

"Your mum is right, Melissa. When I died forty years ago my corpse was frozen cryonically. Your father could confirm it for you because he told me about the system."

Melissa now pretended that she remembered conversations she had had with her father when she was a girl – how she had asked about relatives and how Arthur had told her about her maternal grandfather. She remembered that, if somebody asked about the two men's relationship, she had to say her father had little time for her grandfather. Valerie was keen to intervene at this point because she had noticed her daughter's negative body language. She pulled an old photo from her bag.

"This is your granddad shortly before he died."

She passed the photo to Melissa, who examined it.

The visual likeness was undisputable, so she changed tone both verbally and physically: "It's great to see you, Granddad, because we have never met before."

This was true and for once Joe's emotions took charge; he couldn't say anything, but tears ran down his face.

"I'll get us all a drink; we can have a family celebration."

Valerie's decision helped lower the emotional temperature. Joe and Melissa now sat together on one of the sofas.

"What have you been up to today, Melissa?"

"Please, Granddad, just call me Mel. Melissa is such a gobful. Today I've been fruit picking for hours – there were twelve of us. It was hard work, but I've earned 400 points."

When Valerie returned she immediately raised her eyes to the ceiling grill; sure enough there was now a slight reddish glow in the centre.

Melissa reacted first: "I had a really super day today, Mum; it was good to be picking fruit again."

"Oh, I'm so glad to hear that, Melissa."

Both women turned their gaze upwards; the red glow had vanished.

"Right, Dad, I'll leave you with Mel; I need to attend to Arthur. You can talk freely for now, but keep your eyes on the grill."

When Valerie had left them, Joe smiled at his granddaughter. "Are you married, Mel?"

His granddaughter looked down at her feet for a moment before she replied, "I was, but it didn't last."

"I'm sorry to hear that, Mel, what happened?"

"Well, I'm sure you've spotted that everything in life is now controlled by Vistula, including the one dating agency. Twenty years ago I asked to be introduced to a suitable partner; Vistula Lifestyle agreed. It sent a blob and I was taken to the dating club. There I met John; we got on well. Obviously our conversation was monitored, but we were allowed seven more meetings and then he proposed; we had a civil wedding at the club."

"Were any guests allowed to attend?"

"Oh yes, my parents and John's and other close relatives, like Freddie. After the ceremony John and I entered our own property. The wedding had cost everyone involved a shedload of points.

We all had to work hard to stay in credit. Unfortunately John hated the system and he kicked against it and he was swooped."

"Swooped? What do you mean?"

"The SS came for him; two robots entered our house. They shot him with some kind of torch device and took him away. I've never heard from him again. The next day the Swoop Squad came for me. I was brought here and warned that if I didn't comply with instructions and build up points quickly then I would suffer the same fate as John."

"That's bloody dreadful."

"It's worse than dreadful, Granddad; John and I wanted children, but that process too is controlled by Vistula."

"Surely young people can make love, Mel."

"Yes, if they are married, but if they want a child they have to apply to Vistula Lifestyle. Couples with high points scores are allowed to try for a baby; others, with low scores, like John and me, are turned down."

"But did you attempt to have a child anyway?"

"Yes, but if I had become pregnant I would have been swooped and had to suffer a forced abortion. That was the main reason John rebelled."

"Is there any chance of you meeting another partner?"

"No, Vistula has told me that I must stay here with my parents. Actually I'm not too upset now because, if you become a parent, your child's education is totally directed by the Vistula Education Academy."

"So the child can attend a school, then?"

"Not in the way you remember, Granddad; all lessons are delivered in the house through the screen. Children only learn to read basic English through a system called synthetic phonics – you've possibly picked up how terse all the interactions with Vistula are."

"Yes, I have. Why is that, do you think?"

"I believe there are two reasons. One is the need for the Vistula organisation to have complete power over humans – it allows only a very basic education; it teaches no subject other than basic reading and number recognition. Secondly it needs to conserve electrical power. You will have noticed when you were at Freddie's place that at night no artificial lighting is allowed;

the only exception is a dim glow in the bathroom."

"So do you know how power is generated?"

"Dad told me, before his stroke, that all fossil fuels are banned. A very few atomic power stations remain, but the main power supplies come from natural sources of generation."

"Like wind and tides and sunlight perhaps?"

"That's right, Granddad, and there is one other source that wasn't around in your first life. There's an interesting and amusing story about how it was discovered. Supposedly, about twenty-five years ago, an elderly chap was weeding in his garden; he swiped the head off a weed and noticed that sap spurted out. Later it struck him that two natural forces were in opposition: the downward pressure of gravity against the upward pressure caused by the plant's internal capillary structure. He wondered if the conflict could be used in some way to generate power. No one took any notice to start with, but when global warming became critical it was the Vistula Scientific system which discovered how a weak electric current could be generated from plant life and strengthened so that plants could be used as a source of electrical power."

Joe suddenly remembered all the young evergreen trees he had seen on his travels.

"How does Vistula magnify the power output, Mel?"

"I don't know. Dad might, but unfortunately he can't explain because of his condition; his memory is far from perfect these days, you see, although he does have some lucid periods."

"I suppose Vistula prefers evergreens because they don't shed leaves in the autumn."

"I'm sure that's correct, Granddad."

The red glow appeared again.

Melissa put her finger to her lips before calling through to her mother, "I hope I have to work again tomorrow, Mum, because I need the points."

Valerie didn't reply, but the glow disappeared. Clearly Melissa's statement was considered adequate. It was safe to chat again.

"Granddad, I notice you don't have wrist monitors."

"Freddie tried to register me with Vistula, Mel, but the attempt failed."

"He may have entered something wrong – he's not too good with the technology these days and I bet he hasn't told you the most worrying aspect of life under Vistula."

"What would that be, Mel?"

"Vistula manages life expectancy."

Joe was so shocked he could not take this in.

His granddaughter added more information: "At present no one is allowed to live longer than seventy-eight years; it used to be eighty until a couple of years ago."

"Why the hell is that necessary, Mel?"

"I don't know for sure, but my guess is that since the Great Upheaval the food supply across the world is very limited so one way to manage us humans is to limit our lifespan."

Joe was extremely puzzled.

"But, as you told me a little earlier, couples can still have children."

"Vistula needs young people to carry out some jobs – like the one I had to do today, for example."

"But surely, Mel, its systems are so sophisticated that robots could carry out those simple tasks."

"Yes, you're probably right, but that brings me back to my guess that power generation is a potential problem. As people age they need more care and that means more energy usage."

"So how big is the world population now?"

"There again, Granddad, I don't think any human knows. The Great Upheaval killed millions – probably more than half the world population. The Vistula takeover probably saved what was left of the human race."

Before Joe could react further, the screen burst into life – it was almost time for lights out.

Joe needed to use the bathroom before attempting to sleep. He assumed everybody else was in their bedrooms, so he opened the door and immediately received a great shock: Arthur was sitting on the toilet on top of the closed lid.

"I'm so sorry—" Joe began.

"Turn the cold tap on, Joe, so we can chat."

"I thought you couldn't—"

"Turn the tap on, Joe."

This time Joe carried out the order.

Once the water was flowing Arthur became more vocal: "I have had a stroke, but I've made an almost complete recovery; I still have weakness in my left arm, however, and my memory plays tricks."

"But what about Vistula?"

"For it, I pretend to be worse than I actually am so that hopefully I can find out more about the tyrannous organisation. I bet you've been almost totally bowled over by what has happened since your death."

Joe nodded his agreement.

"I can see from your lack of wrist monitors that you have not been registered. Now you may be completely off the system; on the other hand, Vistula may be aware that there has been a glitch and be actively trying to locate you. I doubt this because the SS would have done a sweep through this property before now."

"Arthur, I can't imagine why it has brought me back to life."

"I can have a guess, Joe: it wanted to find out if its latest medical techniques would work. It uses nanotechnology and probably wanted to test progress. The decision to try to resurrect you would not have been in any way compassionate or to fulfil a legal contract, but purely because Vistula wants to improve its systems. You are a guinea pig, but if it locates you now it will get rid of you pronto, or, of course, it might examine you whilst still living; in that case a second death would be the better option."

Suddenly, without warning, the flow of water stopped. Arthur stood up; he put his right index finger to his lips and beckoned Joe to follow him. He led Joe to his bedroom. Once inside with the door shut, he sat on the bed.

"Sit next to me, Joe, please."

"Is it OK—?"

"Yes, don't worry. After lights out, when the SS thinks everyone is tucked up, all monitoring ceases. Now listen – I'm determined to oppose the situation we find ourselves in, but I need much more information. You could be very useful because you're off the radar."

"It could be very dangerous for me, Arthur."

"Yes indeed, so what I suggest is this: we go one small step at a time."

Joe noted that his son-in-law had changed the singular *I* to the plural *we*, so he repeated his concern: "As I said a moment ago, Arthur, it could be very dangerous for me. Mel has told me what happened to her husband in her presence."

"Yes and Vistula's behaviour like that is one good reason we need to change things, Joe. Now our first small step, as I see it, is this: on a moonlit night, after lights out, you leave the property and have a good look around the immediate area."

"What would I be looking for, do you think, Arthur?"

"Other properties for a start. There may be other persons in your position, and if there are any they may be willing to work with us as a team."

"I can't get my head round how Vistula controls everything, Arthur."

"Well, its systems won't be perfect – you, for instance, are unregistered. Years ago, shortly before you died, a world famous scientist called Professor Stephen Hawking stated that a time would come when no human on the planet would be able to control interconnected computer systems. He was right, and that time came twenty years ago so that now all living humans have to accept Vistula's seemingly absolute power. But, as I said previously, there are sure be weak points, and we, perhaps together with others, need to find them and use them to re-establish human control. Vistula's strongest point is the fact it has power over food supplies and also shelter; these are, as I am sure you appreciate, the basic necessities for human life."

Joe could not disagree. "OK, Arthur, I'll do my best."

"Good man."

CHAPTER 4

Joe had not slept well and his breakfast was not any compensation either. The biscuit thing served today had a slight taste of grapefruit – something that Joe had always avoided since childhood – and the drink had a hint of cold tea. Melissa received a message from Vistula immediately after breakfast and had to leave the property at eight thirty; Arthur remained in his bedroom, presumably asleep, so Joe was left in the company of his daughter.

"There's not much I can offer you, Dad."

"Do we have to stay in here bored to death, then, Val?"

"Well, I can request some entertainment from Vistula Variety, Dad."

"Does it have *Match of the Day*?"

"No team games are allowed these days, Dad – or any other sports, for that matter – but I can request a film if you like."

"I'm sure you remember, Val, that I love science fiction – things like *2001: A Space Odyssey*, for instance."

"We get no choice, Dad; Vistula decides. Shall I do it anyway?"

Joe nodded his acceptance and watched as his daughter entered something on her left wrist monitor, followed shortly by her activating the device on her other wrist. The screen burst into life. The first picture showed the Earth, in full colour, spinning through space.

This was followed by a metallic-sounding voice: "This movie is brought to you by Vistula Variety."

The screen lost its colour and became monochrome. Joe recognised the film's introductory music immediately: he was about to watch Laurel and Hardy in *The Sons of the Desert* – a movie he had first seen when he was an infant. It wasn't new then either.

"Why have—?"

Valerie had an index finger pressed to her lips. Joe looked up to the ceiling – sure enough the grill had a reddish tint.

Valerie smiled and spoke two words in a loud voice: "Oh, good!"

The tint disappeared, but the film didn't. Joe and Valerie watched it in silence. Later his daughter told him that her initial reaction had earned her fifty extra points; she also explained that if she had groaned or made any derogatory remarks she would have had points deducted.

"How do you know your points score, Val?"

"It's quite simple, Dad: I tap my PIN number into my left monitor and when it's accepted I enter a code number into my right monitor. At the moment I have 967 points, which is OK."

"So how do you earn points, then?"

"By complying with all Vistula's requirements. Today, for instance, by staying passive indoors I will be credited with 200 points, but later today the food delivery by drone will cost ninety points, although this will be shared between three of us. Mel will probably earn another 400 working, so we're doing all right. However, things will change dramatically if the SS locates you here; in that case, all of us would be swooped."

This information was enough to leave Joe depressed for the rest of the day.

Melissa returned home earlier than she had the day before, and as she entered the living room the reddish tint glowed in the grill.

"Have you had a good day, darling?"

Melissa smiled before answering her mother's query: "Wonderful, Mum. I love digging up potatoes."

This assessment was enough to extinguish the glow.

"I'll just pop in to see how Dad is today, Mum."

"Righto, darling; I'll get us all a drink."

Arthur did not join the party for the evening biscuits; Melissa took his to him in his bedroom. It seemed that the company was in for a very boring evening.

Valerie attempted to at least stimulate some conversation: "Dad, do you have any more questions? We can watch another ancient film if you like – if we put it on now it will end before lights out."

Joe did not feel up to delving into cinematic history, so he asked a question: "What has happened to world religions, Val? I take it no one can go to church or to a mosque or a temple."

"People can still worship, Dad, but they have to use the screen. Would you like to experience a service?"

Joe had never been religious, but at least a screening would pass some time.

"Yes, OK."

Once again his daughter entered something on her left wrist monitor and after a short pause she switched to that on her right wrist.

The first picture was of the Earth in full colour followed after a few seconds by the metallic voice: "This church service is brought to you by Vistula Culture. Tonight's Anglican service is from St Giles Church in Chelford."

It was clear from the presentation that the service had been recorded before the Great Upheaval. The red glow appeared again in the ceiling grill – both Joe and his daughter noticed it.

"I'm glad it's an Anglican Church service, Mel; what about you?"

Mel, who had now returned from her father's room, immediately recorded her agreement: "Oh yes, Mum, I'm really happy."

The glow disappeared.

Joe paid no heed to the service because he had more questions.

"What if we were Catholic or Muslim?"

Valerie did her best to answer: "My guess is that Vistula knows that I and Arthur attended Protestant services occasionally in the past. We were married in an Anglican church, as I'm sure you recall, and we have attended several family funerals in other Christian churches. Presumably Vistula has information on all persons supporting other religions."

Joe turned to his granddaughter: "But, Mel, you told me that you were married in a Vistula venue."

"That's true, Dad – John and I were quite happy with a civil service and I haven't a clue what would have happened if we had requested a church wedding."

Valerie now attempted to offer her father some further enlightenment: "I'm sure, Dad, that Vistula can offer Catholics or Muslims or Hindus suitable religious events when requested."

The vicar on the screen was now standing in the pulpit ready to start his sermon; the three observers concentrated on him as he began to speak.

"I want to concentrate today on the beginning of life here on Earth as set out in Genesis. Verse one states that God formed heaven and Earth on the first day; well, science later found out that a day is defined by a single rotation of the Earth on its axis, but at the start of the Creation there was no day because the Earth hadn't yet been formed. Much later scientists put forward other concepts like the Big Bang theory, which they reckon happened 13.8 billion years ago – an event that is now recognised as the true birth of our universe. Now, which should we believe – the guesswork of Genesis or the scientific explanation? Vistula, our grand saviour, leaves it an open question for you all to ponder. In the New Testament Jesus rises from His tomb in bodily form to confront Doubting Thomas, one of His disciples. Was this a possibility for someone who had been crucified? He would have needed a beating heart and blood coursing through His body, but surely this was impossible bearing in mind the fact that He had five holes punched into His flesh. Vistula leaves you to mull over this circumstance and please take into account that nowadays modern technology can fashion intelligent robots which can carry out all life's essential functions without end; perhaps this is the true Resurrection."

Finally a choir of mainly mature persons sang 'Abide with Me'.

When it was over Joe offered a comment: "Surely we should have sung 'Abide with Vistula'."

It was quite clear to him that the recorded service had been doctored to support Vistula's total control.

The red glow reappeared.

Mel noticed and reacted first: "What a wonderful service! It was so thought-provoking."

Her mother agreed: "Yes indeed, darling."

When the glow had faded Joe offered more comments: "That was very interesting. Clearly Vistula has recorded and amended a genuine church service filmed several years ago to promote its position."

Melissa agreed with him: "Yes, Granddad, it's all part of its need to control everything."

Just before lights out Joe visited the bathroom; once again he encountered Arthur, who seemed fully awake.

"Have you had an interesting day, Joe?"

"No, not really. I watched an ancient film which I had seen years ago – I didn't really find it amusing then – and this evening Val found a church service for us all to watch."

"You were never religious, as I remember, in your previous life."

"That's true, but it was interesting for me to see Vistula's take on the Church of England."

"Were you impressed?"

"No, I was confused because it seemed as though Vistula was casting doubt on Christianity without being too autocratic."

"Like you, Joe, I have only ever watched one service and I came to a similar conclusion. Years ago religion was an important part of many people's existence. The various faiths gave worshippers hope, a sense of identity and a code for living in harmony; unfortunately all faiths also whipped up divisions and conflict, so that now, I guess, after the Great Upheaval, which no human action could control, Vistula is trying to divert people to its more scientific view."

"Is it succeeding, would you say, Arthur?"

"Please remember, Joe, that the Great Upheaval almost obliterated the human race. Vistula is now totally in control – and that needs opposing, as I know you agree, so tonight, which is cloudless and with a full moon, you could make a short reconnaissance. Are you willing to give it a go?"

"Yes, OK, but I'm not going far – I don't want to get lost and swooped by the SS."

"There's no chance of the latter after lights out, but I agree that you should stay close to this property. Just get your bearings and report anything you consider important to me. I'll let you out, and don't worry – I'll make sure you can re-enter this property."

Joe was shaking a little as he left the property, but the bright moonlight eventually gave him enough confidence to walk to the roadway – a distance of about twenty metres ahead. He was surprised by the road's surface, which appeared pale grey in the moonlight. He bent forward to touch it and found that is was composed of small, flattened, elliptical pieces which felt like plastic. He wondered which way to turn. The moon was shining from his left, so he turned that way. After walking for about two minutes he saw a dome-shaped building on his right. It was similar in shape to Arthur's property, but was decidedly smaller; there was no sign of life, so he walked on. After another couple of minutes he saw a similar building on his left set back from the roadway; this too was smaller than Arthur's. It was about thirty metres back from the road, and again there was no sign of life. Joe decided to continue onwards for a few more minutes. Suddenly a cloud covered the moon and darkness enveloped him. He stood stock-still praying the light would return; fortunately the cloud soon passed over and Joe could see again.

He was about to retrace his steps when something caught his eye over to his right. He edged forward to gain a better view. As he approached he almost gasped out loud because he was nearing the biggest building he had ever seen. It was rectangular and, though it wasn't high, it stretched out of view. The nearest thing he could equate it to, from his previous life, was a supermarket depot he had once seen from a motorway. That, however, was dwarfed by this monstrosity. There seemed to be a parking area to one side. Joe took a few steps in that direction. There were no cars or trucks, or even a fence, but literally hundreds of drones. Some were small, others very much larger. Joe would have approached closer, but a movement from somewhere close behind him in the undergrowth startled him. Was it the SS?

Joe didn't hang about – he turned and ran in the direction of Arthur's property. He was in luck because he arrived back safely just before a storm cloud totally obliterated the moonlight.

Arthur had kept his word and Joe had no problem entering the property. He turned towards his bedroom, but was prevented because Arthur appeared before him.

"Come to my room, Joe – I want to hear about your outing."

When they were both sitting Arthur spoke again: "Right, Joe – I'd like to hear everything in detail right from the beginning."

Joe took a deep breath. "I went straight to the roadway after leaving this property."

Arthur knew this to be true because he had watched Joe's first steps from the door.

"I was surprised by the road's covering, so I bent down to examine it; it seemed to be formed from small pieces of plastic."

"Well, you see, Joe, plastic has become a very important component of many things these days. You might remember in your first life that the seas, oceans, rivers and landfill were full of the stuff. The Great Upheaval killed off many life forms, but it did not affect plastic in any way. The country which was then called Holland was the first nation to use recycled plastic beads on a cycle track, and now Vistula has learned how to use plastic in many other ways as well – roads are only one of them. This property, for instance, is composed almost entirely of plastic."

Joe was confused and interrupted: "I remember the problems with plastic in my first life, Arthur, and, as I recall, there were many different types, of which only some could be recycled."

"That was true then, Joe, but now all forms can be recycled thanks to a breakthrough brought about by Vistula. This house is pinned to the ground using some steel, but most of its structure is plastic-based. It is dome-shaped because plastic can be worked more easily in that form. Glass is not allowed any more, but the screen in every home compensates for the lack of windows. Now tell me more about your outing."

Joe recounted everything he could remember, laying particular stress on the huge depot-like building. Arthur did not appear to be impressed.

"That place will probably be where food and drink are manufactured; many of the drones you saw will bring fresh produce to the building, which in fact is also a local depot. The smaller drones deliver the finished product to each household; this ensures, of course, that no one starves – as long as they play by the rules, that is. It's another example of Vistula's almost total control, and that needs changing. I would love a plate of steak and chips. Now, did you experience anything else and why did you decide to return here at the time you did?"

"When I was approaching the huge depot I sensed something behind me; I didn't have a clue what it was, so I skedaddled back here."

"You saw nothing, then?"

"No, I suppose it could have been an animal – like a fox, for instance."

"Unlikely, Joe, but interesting nevertheless. I have trawled through the Vistula Lifestyle Meteorology section and found that tomorrow night will also be cloud-free. Are you willing to do another reconnaissance?"

"Yes, a short one."

"Good. Turn right after leaving the property, Joe, just to see if there are any more huge depots. Now I'm sure you're feeling tired, so I'll say goodnight. You can lie in tomorrow."

CHAPTER 5

It was very late when Joe awoke. Melissa was still at home, but on this particular day Valerie had been summoned to work; there was no sign of Arthur.

"Is your father OK, Mel?"

"His health fluctuates after his stroke, Granddad, but he is very sensible and I guess that today he knows he needs extra rest."

"Do you know where Val is?"

"No. She was picked up by a really big blob early this morning; she had to take all our dirty uniforms with her, so I guess she'll be washing clothes."

"Surely some of Vistula's robots could do that, Mel."

"I'm sure you're right, but it will be a way of maintaining control over humans and saving electric power. Your uniform will need washing soon. Normally we leave our dirty clothes outside the property when ordered to by Vistula Lifestyle; they are picked up be a drone sometime in the day and replaced by a clean set. Obviously today there could be problems."

"So you don't own your clothing, then?"

"We own nothing; everything is supplied by Vistula, which can withdraw anything or indeed everything if we don't follow instructions."

"Surely people protest."

"There is no way to protest. Our wrist monitors will accept questions, but if we make any negative statements they are immediately deleted as are any attempted orders we might try. Vistula will only react to queries and requests. You must remember, Granddad, that our lives depend solely on its systems."

As if to back this up, the screen burst into life; the metallic voice spoke: "It is time for your daily exercise. Ready, and squat."

Joe watched in amazement as his granddaughter was ordered to carry out various movements. Finally, after half an hour, the voice announced the end of the session.

"Well done. You have earned fifty points."

'Yes,' Joe thought to himself. 'Yes, indeed, the regime must be changed.'

It was another boring day. Melissa noticed her grandfather's negative mood.

"Would you like to read a story, Granddad?"

"Oh, yes please. Do you have books?"

"No, but I can put in a request on the system."

"OK, then. Now, I love science fiction."

"Vistula will decide, Granddad, and remember it will know I'm making the request so the subject matter may not be of much interest to you."

It wasn't, and Joe found himself forced to listen to a story about a heroic robot combating a pride of lions. Of course the robot came out on top – the lions all perished and, in a stroke of propaganda, the last two utterances made clear that all nature was now totally controlled by Vistula and that all humans were safe as long as they obeyed orders.

"Did you enjoy the story, Granddad?"

"No, not at all. How many points did it cost you?"

"Fifty."

Valerie returned home at five o'clock. She was obviously worn out, but she made sure that, when the grill glowed red, she made an appropriate comment.

"I've had the most fulfilling day, Mel."

"I'm so pleased for you, Mum."

The glow faded.

Valerie slumped on to the settee and told the others her real assessment: "We had to wash hundreds of uniforms in a very old-fashioned way. First we filled huge vats with hot water, which we hand to carry in buckets from a heated tank; then we poured in some evil-smelling washing powder. My job was to operate a posser."

"A what, Mum?"

"A posser, Mel. It's a long stick thing with a flat circular structure on the end. I had to move it up and down violently in the vat so it loosened any dirt. I did that for five hours."

"How many points did you earn, Val?"

"I'm not sure, Dad, but I can find out."

She operated her two wrist monitors before announcing that her efforts meant she had earned 200 points. Melissa was about to complain, but stopped herself in time because the red glow was evident again.

Later, just before lights out, Arthur summoned Joe to his room.

"Right, Joe, are you ready for your next outing?"

"Yes, I am. My poor daughter has had one hell of a day."

Without another word Joe left the property and, as arranged, tonight he turned right. For the first ten minutes or so Joe thought his reconnaissance would be even less successful than his previous outing. He saw a couple of properties; both were smaller than Arthur's. Reluctantly he continued on the pale plastic road for another ten minutes or so, but then, just as he was about to retrace his steps, something large and jagged caught his attention. Cautiously he stepped off the roadway and made his way through the undergrowth towards the site. He nearly tripped over something thin and cord-like, but managed somehow to stay upright. He looked down and was amazed to find there was now tarmac under his feet; the surface was uneven and rutted, but it was undoubtedly part of a former road.

He was now nearing his target and he could see old-fashioned brick and concrete buildings; all of them were badly damaged. As he walked on he noticed a buckled sign lying in the undergrowth; it was pointing upwards from its horizontal position and the moonlight allowed Joe to read the name 'Chelford'. He had found the town where he had lived as a lad after the breakdown of his parents' relationship. Now he was able to make connections, despite the damage. He was in what was left of the High Street; the Grosvenor Public House was on his right. Further on to his left was all that remained of the town's best restaurant – he was able to make out its name on a battered signpost: 'The Olive ree'. It had obviously lost its second letter T. He hadn't lost his memory, however. He now remembered that he and Margaret used to eat at the restaurant most weekends; they had become firm friends with the owners, Martino and Louisa. Both Joe and Margaret loved the laid-back ambience and the delicious tapas dishes. Joe put such memories aside and forced himself to concentrate on the present.

A huge pile of damaged brickwork forced him to turn right where he encountered what was left of the town's market cross. Joe knew he was now in the former Church Street. As he looked ahead the most saddening sight so far came into view. Since the mid nineteenth century Chelford had boasted one of the most impressive churches in Britain. The original neo-Gothic building had been designed by Augustus Pugin, an Anglo-French architect. Once its pointed spire had dominated the surrounding area; tonight it lay scattered and battered over the churchyard, and no doubt in neighbouring streets. One of the famous Pugin doors, with its rampant red lion, was propped upright against a gravestone; next to it were the remains of the school Joe had attended as an infant. It was where he had first met Rodney Salt – they had often sat next to each other. Joe now brought to mind some of their teachers – the formidable Miss Forsdyke and the head teacher, Mr Noakes – the lollipop lady, Maggie Sims, and the often tasteless school dinners.

He remembered his first day in the reception class. At playtime he needed to wee, but, as he didn't know where the toilets were, he performed in a corner of the playground. Rodney Salt joined him and both of them were caught and had to appear before Mr Noakes. They both expected to be told off and were surprised when the head teacher almost smiled when told about their escapade by Miss Forsdyke; she, however, was definitely not amused.

Time was passing, so once again Joe attempted to stop his mind from being overwhelmed by the past. All those people would probably now be dead and modern children, under Vistula's rule, were being denied direct learning alongside their peers. Joe recognised that if the present situation was allowed to continue all human life would be reduced to serfdom. This situation further strengthened his resolve to do something positive.

By now the moonlight was fading. Joe turned and started to return to Arthur, but as he turned out of Church Street he heard something behind him. He turned quickly and caught a glimpse of a person flitting across the graveyard. Was it the SS? Joe didn't hang about – he took off. He was breathless when he arrived back at the property. Arthur had left the door open for him, so he staggered in.

"Are you all right, Joe?"

He took a deep breath before answering Arthur's question: "I saw someone, Arthur; it was definitely a person, probably female."

"Where were you when this happened?"

"I had found the town where I was brought up – you know, Chelford."

"Are you absolutely certain?"

"Yes, yes, I recognised the ruins of many buildings, including my old infant school and the Gothic church, and I found a town sign. I thought the SS was after me."

"Just calm yourself, Joe, because if it had really been the SS we wouldn't be having this conversation. I think it's good news you saw someone because, I guess, they're almost definitely in the same position as you are and they won't be alone. Now what I suggest is this: you return tomorrow night because we need to make contact with other outcasts like you – yes, and me as well," he added quickly.

"Are you willing to come with me tomorrow, Arthur?"

"I'd really like to, Joe, but my stroke has left me weak on the left side and I can't really walk any distance. Now, I'll tell you what – if you do make contact, invite the person or persons here so we can discuss ways forward."

"You're making a big assumption there, Arthur."

"Yes, yes, I recognise that, but I feel sure that others share our opinions of Vistula and I don't want to see your daughter put under the stress she suffered earlier today, do you?"

Joe felt he had to agree with the second part of Arthur's statement. He needed rest, so he turned to leave.

"We can discuss our next moves tomorrow, Joe. Goodnight."

Was that birdsong that had awakened him? Joe sat up in bed. He heard the sound again – yes, he decided, it was definitely a chaffinch. In his youth Joe had been a member of a birdwatching group, but this was the first time in his second life that he had heard any animal noise apart from the rustle in the undergrowth near the huge depot. He got out of bed immediately, dressed hurriedly and entered the main room, where he found his daughter and granddaughter eating their breakfast biscuits.

"I've just heard a chaffinch," he told them.

Melissa smiled at him and pointed to the screen.

Joe turned his head to look; he was confronted by a woodland scene and on one branch there was a cock chaffinch. As if on cue, the bird opened its beak and sang.

"We thought you'd like to be awakened with birdsong, Dad. Here's your breakfast biscuit, by the way."

Joe spent another boring day despite his close relatives' attempts to interest him with programmes shown on the screen, like a Charlie Chaplin film and physical exercises. Despite his fears, he decided that he would make another trip to what was left of Chelford – anything was better than daily boredom. He was actually grateful when night came and he could leave the property.

"It will be more overcast tonight, Joe, so be extra-careful."

"Well, Arthur, I know the way and once I get to Chelford I'll find the spot where I first saw the person."

"Good man, Joe. Try to communicate and remember you can always invite whoever it is back here while it's lights out."

Outside it was decidedly blustery; the moonlight flickered like a bulb on its last legs. Nevertheless Joe continued his walk. He took some time to find the place where he had to leave the plastic track, and when he reached the shattered town it was a good job his memory was still in working order. He walked down Church Street towards the damaged building and found what he estimated to be the spot from where he had seen the fleeting image. A cloud covered the moon. Joe stood stock-still and waited for the moonlight to return. When it did he climbed over a partly demolished wall into the graveyard. He paused for a moment or two behind a large leaning tombstone; the moonlight disappeared again. Suddenly he felt something pressing into his back.

"Do not move." The voice was menacing and high-pitched.

Joe froze. Had the SS got him? he wondered. The moon

reappeared; there standing before him was a human person.

"Hold out both arms now!"

Joe followed the order immediately.

"It's OK, Emma, he's got no wrist monitors."

Joe felt the pressure on his back ease.

"Come with us; do not speak."

Joe followed the human who had confronted him, while being aware that there was someone or something close behind him. The threesome walked across the graveyard towards the remains of the church. Suddenly the first human stopped. The moonlight went again, and when it reappeared Joe found himself facing some steps leading downwards.

Now, for the second time, he heard the voice from behind his back: "Go down now."

Once again Joe followed an order.

He counted eight steps before he found himself in a dimly lit crypt.

"Sit there."

At last, in the dim candlelight, he could see something of one of his captors. She was an elderly woman with grey hair and dark skin; she was not wearing a Vistula uniform, but a grey jacket and bluish slacks.

"Who are you?"

"My name is Joseph Fenton."

This answer elicited a gasp of surprise and, for the first time, the human behind him came into his line of sight.

"I know him, Flora – he is Joseph Fenton."

"How can you be so sure, Emma?"

"Because we met a few times many years ago when I was his son's partner. Still playing the field, is he, Joe?"

Joe gazed at the woman, searching his long-term memory. The trouble was that Freddie had had so many partners during Joe's previous life.

The woman tried to help him: "Your wife was called Margaret and you lived on a large estate on the Staffordshire moorlands."

At last something clicked in Joe's brain.

"Yes, I remember you now – you're Emma Cross."

"What are you doing here?" The dark woman posed the question.

"I might ask you two the same," Joe retorted.

"You first, Joe." Emma made the invitation in a softer tone than her colleague.

"I've been resurrected, Emma."

"Stop being stupid and answer my question."

Joe looked up at the one called Flora, his first inquisitor. "Look – I died over forty years ago, but I paid for my body to be preserved until such time as the cancer that killed me could be cured. I was brought back to life a short time ago by Vistula."

"I very much doubt that."

Emma now stepped in: "He's telling the truth, Flora, because, many years ago, I remember my mother reading about a special church service dedicated to the memory of Joseph Fenton. If he hadn't died he would now be in his nineties and Vistula would have eliminated him. He looks now just as I remember him all those years ago."

The one called Flora had more queries. She looked at Emma. "Why would Vistula bother?"

"I guess it will be something to do with genetic engineering; as we both know, Vistula is trying to reduce human brainpower and by resurrecting Joe they will be looking to extend their knowledge and powers over us humans."

Flora wasn't convinced. "But why isn't he locked away, then?"

Joe intervened at this point: "I think I know why. When I was brought back to life I was taken to my son's property; he was supposed to register me with Vistula Lifestyle, but something went wrong – some glitch or other. That's why I don't have wrist monitors. Freddie took me to his sister's place, near here."

"Has anyone there tried to register you?" Once again it was Flora asking the probing question.

"No, in fact my son-in-law is an opponent of Vistula; he wants to see us humans taking back power."

Emma's memory had clicked into gear again. "I can recall your son-in-law, a stuck-up bloke called Arthur."

"Yes, that's right, Emma. He lives with my daughter, Valerie, and my grandchild, Melissa."

"He must have a larger-than-normal property, then."

"Yes, he does, Flora. Evidently he was one of the people who helped Vistula rise to eminence, so it rewarded him." Joe could see from Flora's face that she still wasn't convinced, so he added more detail: "He had a stroke sometime ago, so he needs extra care. Perhaps that's the reason."

"Vistula is not noted for compassion, is it, Emma?"

"No, it isn't."

"Well, ladies, in my opinion he is quite genuine; so are his aims. In fact, he will be pleased to meet both of you."

"We are not the only ones opposing the system, Joe; there are several others."

"Are they here in Chelford, Emma?"

"Not full-time. You see, we have to forage for food; we can all find shelter in the ruins, but food is a problem. Often we hide out near properties so that when the drones deliver we take the food before the inhabitants pick it up. We have to be very, very careful – two of our colleagues have been swooped by the SS so far."

"But surely it's OK after lights out, because Arthur told me that everything is shut down."

Emma shook her head. "Not everything, Joe. Drones with heat-sensitive night vision still patrol."

"Are you sure about that, Emma?"

"Absolutely – just listen."

Joe shut up and concentrated; sure enough he heard a faint swishing sound, which gradually grew louder. He was tempted to climb the steps and look out, but Flora grabbed his arm.

"We must stay hidden – it will have heat monitors and infrared cameras."

The noise continued at the same pitch. Clearly the drone was hovering somewhere near, but after two or three minutes the sound faded.

"Now are you convinced, Joe?"

He nodded his agreement.

Emma looked outside. "It's getting late, Joe – I suggest you go now. The drone won't return till daylight, but keep your ears open and walk at the edge of the track so you can dive into the undergrowth."

"Right – thanks, Emma. I'll tell Arthur of our meeting."

"Yes, please do, and also ask him to visit us."

"Right – bye for now."

Joe left the crypt and made his way back to his family. The

door was ajar so Joe could enter easily; Arthur was waiting to talk.

"Anything interesting, Joe?"

"Yes, indeed. I met two women in the churchyard and I knew one of them from my first life; you may have met her too, Arthur. Her name is Emma Cross – she was one of Freddie's numerous girlfriends."

"I can't say I recognise the name, Joe, but carry on."

"The other woman is called Flora; she seemed to be in charge."

"Are there any other free spirits, Joe?"

"Yes, but I didn't meet them. They were foraging for food."

"Did the women say where?"

"No, but the whole group is opposed to Vistula."

"I'd like to meet all or just some of them. Could that be arranged, do you think?"

"Probably, Arthur, but I think they'd prefer to meet you on their terms; however, I did mention your stroke."

"Did they mention any ideas for breaking the Vistula system?"

"No, not really."

"Right. Now, if you can, meet them again and definitely invite them here."

"I'll do that, Arthur, but now I'm feeling knackered, so goodnight."

Flora and Emma had put their heads together when Joe had left the crypt.

"Can we use him, do you think, Emma?"

"Well, what he told us about his rebirth is certainly genuine in my view."

"But are you 100 per cent certain he's not being set up by Vistula?"

"Ninety-nine per cent, Flora. And consider this: we all agree that one way to overcome Vistula is to hack into its system, but we have no means of access; however, I'm sure Joe's son-in-law will have because he'll have wrist monitors and possibly enough knowledge to do some damage."

"OK, Emma, we'll discuss our next moves when the other guys return."

It was almost daylight when the group's two other members returned from their foraging. Pete Mitchell and Justin Brown had had some success – they had two breakfast biscuits and a few eating apples which they had found on a lone tree. Flora told them immediately every detail of their meeting with Joe Fenton. They listened intently. Justin, a former biologist, knew about cryonics.

"It is perfectly feasible that Vistula has enough knowledge and technique to have brought this guy back to life. It is also feasible that Vistula has brainwashed him. What do you think, Pete?"

"We've got to be very careful, but there is a chance that this Arthur bloke is genuine and can help us hack into the system, so I suggest this: one of us stays here tomorrow night in case Fenton shows up again." He turned to Emma: "You do it, Emma, because Fenton will trust you." He turned back to the others: "We three must wait in hiding until Emma judges that it really is Fenton and not some imposter; then she brings him to join us, but not here."

"Where do you suggest, then, Pete?"

"In the basement of The Olive Tree restaurant, Flora."

"Why there?"

"Just in case Vistula manages to observe Fenton's arrival. We need to let him enter the crypt alone under our surveillance, then, after a few minutes, if we are convinced all is safe, Emma goes to join him and engage him in conversation so she can establish without doubt that he really is Joseph Fenton and not some robot in disguise. As I said earlier, we have to be very careful."

No one present disagreed with him.

CHAPTER 6

Joe awoke with a jerk – someone was tugging his left arm.

"Wake up, Dad. Mel and I have to work; the blob will pick us up in five minutes. I've left your biscuit and liquid out for breakfast. Arthur is awake – he'll keep you company. I'll see you later."

"Where are you off to, Val?"

"I haven't a clue, but it's the first time both Mel and I have been called out together."

Valerie left the bedroom; Joe was faced with another boring day. He got up, put on his overall and went to the main room. To his surprise Arthur was sitting on the sofa.

"I thought you might want to watch something on the screen, Joe."

"I'm OK, Arthur, thanks. I've just had a dream – now, that's one thing Vistula can't control."

"Absolutely right, Joe. When I was a student I studied some research on dreaming – the process is essential for our mental health. One researcher found out that there are different stages of sleep. One stage he called rapid eye movement or REM sleep; when he woke people up in this stage they were almost always dreaming. His next step was to wake people up when REM sleep began, but he had to end the experiments because people became confused; some even had hallucinations. What was your dream about?"

"I dreamt I was swimming in the sea; a large wave pushed me under the surface and I came face-to-face with a huge fish. It was coming towards me with its mouth open, but then Val woke me up. I haven't a clue what the dream was about – I can't swim and I know very little about fish."

"I don't think dreaming has any messages for us, Joe. Our senses

111

are shut down when we sleep, so the brain has a free range."

"But surely, Arthur, our senses of smell and hearing are still working so our dreams may be influenced by a limited sensory input. I guess Vistula's systems must have limited input too, and I've come to believe that it is under human control – probably by some megalomaniac who is extremely rich with at least four yachts and his own island."

"I doubt that, Joe. The Great Upheaval allowed Vistula to take over completely – I know that for certain because the firm I worked for helped Vistula develop its systems, which over the last twenty years will have become even more sophisticated; it will use three-dimensional modelling, for instance."

"I bet its systems are not totally secure because Freddie was not able to register me, was he?"

"Ah, Freddie – not the brightest spark, eh, Joe?"

"Just remember, Arthur, that he had plenty of business acumen. You can possibly recall that he had a contract with that global firm Herculeum."

Arthur recognised at this point that the former bad feeling between him and his father-in-law could return, so he changed the subject: "Do you feel OK about tonight, Joe?"

"Yes, I'll chance it again, and tonight I could well meet some other dissenters. The two I have met so far are keen to meet you, but on their ground, not here. I have explained about your health, but I'll offer them an invitation again."

"Good, Joe. Tell them that I have access to Vistula, which they can observe while I attempt to explain its systems; that might do the trick."

To the men's surprise both Valerie and Melissa rejoined them before lunch.

"What did you have to do today, ladies?"

Valerie answered her father: "Sweeping up leaves. There weren't too many, thank goodness."

Joe wasn't surprised because it was clear from his outings that evergreens were more in abundance than deciduous trees.

"We've earned 200 points each," Melissa informed the men.

Arthur went to bed after lunch; Melissa helped him to his room, leaving Joe with his daughter.

"What strange lives we have to lead nowadays, Val, but how can we change things?"

"I haven't a clue, Dad, but all things do change over time."

"Yes, you're right, but can interactive computer systems, over which humans have no control, continue to develop indefinitely? Surely things wear out and need replacement, so there must be pressure on essentials like plastic, metals and power sources. Personally I doubt that the situation we are in can continue to infinity."

"I really can't get to grips with the concept of infinity, Dad; I just worry about whether we have enough food. Now would you like to hear some music for a change?"

Valerie's offer was better than total sedentary boredom, so Joe agreed. Once again he watched as his daughter operated her wrist monitors.

"Can I request some jazz, Val?"

"I'll try, Dad, but Vistula Variety will make the decision."

To Joe's immense surprise a vocalist – one his grandmother adored years ago – began to sing. He hadn't heard Johnny Mathis since his childhood. It wasn't exactly jazz, but it was close. Joe spent the rest of the afternoon listening to what used to be called the Great American Songbook, and for the first time since his resurrection he felt truly relaxed.

His sense of relaxation lasted till twilight, when, once again, Arthur invited him into the bedroom.

"Tell your contacts, Joe, that I have been able to download some of Vistula's systems, which they need to examine; however, to do that at least one of them will have to accompany you here."

"OK, Arthur, I'll try. Do you happen to know how Vistula develops its power? It seems to me it can create the birth of new systems. Are there male and female algorithms, for example?"

"That's a good question, Joe. I guess they're all neuter and that all developments are based on collected, analysed data. Remember Vistula came to prominence when the human race was under severe threat; it saved what was left of the world by analysing essential data – for instance, climate, food sources, raw materials and suchlike. It communicated with the remaining humans at the time and then took the lead in establishing routes to survival. Obviously by now it has gone too far, and I'm pleased there are people out there who want to change things. Right, Joe, it's almost lights out so please get ready for your next meeting and remember to tell them about my progress in cracking the Vistula systems."

For the third consecutive night Joe made his way to the ruins of Chelford. He found the crypt easily and entered. To his immense surprise he found himself alone. What should he do? he wondered. He didn't want to risk being detected by a drone, but, on the other hand, he didn't want to spend all the night in the darkened crypt. He was still pondering on this when a shadow fell across the entrance. Joe looked around desperately for a hiding place. He heard someone or something come down the steps.

"I know you're in here, Joe."

To his immense relief he came face to face with Emma Cross.

"I thought you'd be here waiting for me, Emma."

"You know we have to be extra careful, Joe. Has Arthur made any progress today?"

"Yes, he told me earlier this evening that he can log on to at least one of the Vistula systems."

This information was enough to convince Emma that the male with her was the genuine article.

"Tonight, Joe, we're meeting at another venue – please follow me."

She led him across what was left of Queen Street into the equally damaged Chapel Street and finally into the former High Street. The moon appeared fleetingly and Joe recognised their destination was to be The Olive Tree restaurant. Emma manipulated herself around smashed brickwork and burned timbers to a stairwell leading downwards.

At last she turned to Joe: "We've made it; now follow me down so you can meet the others."

The stairs were steep, and to complicate things they turned through forty-five degrees; however, there was some light so that, when Joe arrived in the basement, he could make out three faces illuminated by candlelight.

He immediately recognised Flora, who stood up and spoke: "Welcome, Joe. Now I'd like you to meet two new colleagues." She pointed to a male on her left. "This is Pete and over there is Justin."

Joe nodded at both men, who reciprocated in similar fashion.

Emma now took the lead: "Flora and I have told the guys all about you, Joe, and they are both interested in your links with your son-in-law."

It took some time for Joe's eyesight to cope with the limited light which came from a single candle set upright on an old cracked saucer. He looked again at the two males. The one called Pete was standing before him; he was tall and extremely thin. The other was seated on a bench; he looked to be the older of the two.

Joe spoke softly and directed his words towards the men: "I left Arthur – that's my son-in-law – earlier. He is keen to meet you because he shares your views on Vistula. Unfortunately he couldn't accompany me because of his health – I'm sure the ladies have mentioned his stroke. He worked for Vistula years ago in a senior capacity and therefore has some knowledge of their systems."

Justin raised a doubt at this point: "But, as you've just said, that was years ago, wasn't it? So he has no up-to-date knowledge, then."

"Yes, that's true, Justin, but he has wrist monitors so he can connect to Vistula's systems; he reckons he can hack into at least one. Now, if one or all of you could meet him, working together you might gain insights into how to hack into more of them."

Joe looked at the four candlelit faces.

Flora reacted first: "Right – what I suggest is this: one of us goes with you tonight, Joe, to meet this Arthur just to make an initial contact, and I suggest Pete is the man for the job; he's the fittest and in his working life he worked for a time as a website designer. I realise of course that was years ago, but it seems the best way forward for me."

She looked around the basement.

Joe sought to back her up: "If Pete comes with me now he can return safely within the lights-out period."

All eyes turned to Pete, who agreed with the suggestion: "That's fine with me, Joe, so come on – let's get going."

For the first time since his return from the dead Joe found himself taking the lead. It was dark, but he recognised enough of the former Chelford street system to locate the plastic road. Pete followed closely behind him. It took them fifteen minutes or so to arrive at the property. Pete was surprised to find the door open.

Once inside, Joe made his way to Arthur's room – that door was also open. Joe tapped on it and entered. Arthur was propped up in bed.

"I've brought a guest to see you, Arthur. His name is Pete and he's keen to discuss ways to outwit Vistula."

"Well, hi, Pete. Great to meet you."

Pete did not exchange any pleasantries; he came straight to the point: "Joe tells me you are able to hack into Vistula's systems."

"That is correct, Pete, and of course I have direct contact with the organisation. This evening I've managed to enter several of their systems."

"Did you find any weaknesses?"

"No, but I have an idea. You see, from time to time Vistula sends a couple of robots to check on my health, so I have requested a visit tomorrow."

"How will that help, Arthur?"

"Well, Joe, I'll tell them I'm very weak and have a pain in my chest. They will seek medical guidance using their monitors; I will watch like a hawk to find out how they connect with the appropriate system. I know it's not much, but it's a start, and then, if I can meet Pete's colleagues here tomorrow night, we can try various ideas using my monitors to enter and possibly cause havoc in at least one of Vistula's systems. One thing is absolutely certain: their algorithms will have a weakness or even weaknesses somewhere, and with six minds working together with the same aim I'm sure we can hack into at least one. Now, what do you think?"

Pete did not reply straight away. Joe was delighted to note that Arthur had included him in the six minds.

Finally, after what seemed like a slice of infinity, Pete spoke: "What I'll do is this: I'll return to my colleagues now and report what you have told me. Send Joe to Chelford tomorrow after lights out to find out our joint decision. Now I must leave – it's getting late."

With that, Pete turned and left.

Once he was out of the property Arthur smiled at Joe. "Well done – now we're really getting somewhere."

"Have you really asked for a visit from the robots?"

"Oh yes. Actually, Joe, they're not the most sophisticated part of Vistula, in my view, but while they're here you must stay hidden, of course."

Pete returned directly to the restaurant. He had a slight problem finding the point where to leave the plastic roadway, but fortunately the moon shone briefly and he was able to locate the exact spot. His three colleagues were still in the basement.

"What's your assessment of this Arthur, then, Pete?"

"Well, Flora, I think he's genuine. He certainly has two wrist monitors and he has a plan which may help us. Tomorrow he's requested help from two robots who monitor his health condition; he will scrutinise their methods of connecting with Vistula and make a mental note. At the next lights out he suggests Joe Fenton returns here to take us to his property so we can use his findings, and, as a team, seek to hack into Vistula."

Flora had her doubts: "OK, but we'd be leaving ourselves open to detection."

Justin had a different view: "Look, Flora – we can't keep on living like this. We've returned to the hunter-gatherer stage of human development, and as we all know we don't have much success in either hunting or gathering, so surely we must take this chance. None of us is getting physically stronger or younger."

"How about a vote, Flora?"

"Good idea, Justin. Hands up all those who wish to meet this Arthur."

Emma and the two men raised their hands.

"Right – you three win, and as a true democrat I'll accept your vote and come with you."

Flora's statement had an immediate detrimental effect on the candle, which went out leaving a whiff of smoke in the air.

Joe slept well right through the night until his granddaughter woke him.

"I've brought your breakfast, Granddad. I'm very sorry, but you'll have to stay in this room till the robots have finished with Dad. I suggest you get some more shut-eye after your breakfast. Mum has sent you her drink today. Later I'll let you know when the coast is clear."

Joe sat up in bed and nibbled through his biscuit, which today had a muesli-like taste, before drinking the liquid. It seemed stronger than normal and an orange tang was very noticeable. Joe knew he was faced with yet more boredom, but this morning he felt very tired and within minutes he went back to sleep.

He must have slept a long time because when he finally awoke it was twilight. 'Surely Arthur's visitors would have left by now.' This thought was confirmed when Val entered the room.

"OK, Dad, you can come to the main room now; the robots have left."

Joe was surprised to find that Arthur wasn't in the main room with Melissa and Valerie.

"Is Arthur OK?"

"No worries, Dad. He gets very tired when the robots visit."

"Have you two had to work today?"

"No, Dad, it was important that we both stayed close to Arthur."

"Is he fit enough to meet people?"

Valerie assured her father that her husband was just having a nap and was eagerly looking forward to the meeting.

"Right, ladies, I'll go and fetch them."

By now Joe was confident he knew the route. Even in the dark he found the way into what passed these days for Chelford town centre, but there he had a problem: where would the dissidents be waiting? He decided to approach what was left of the restaurant.

Emma settled his confusion: "We're all here, Joe."

Sure enough four vague shapes appeared from the restaurant's ruins.

"This way, folks," Joe announced as he turned to retrace his steps.

No one spoke a word on the walk. Pete Mitchell brought up the rear; Emma stayed close behind Joe, with Justin and Flora sandwiched between her and Pete. The door was open when they arrived at the property, so they entered the main room together. Joe was surprised that nobody was there to meet them.

"Take a seat, folks, while I find Arthur."

Joe went to the door of Arthur's room and tapped on it.

"We're all here, Arthur."

There was a short pause before Arthur appeared at the threshold; he was dressed in the normal grey uniform.

"Right Joe, introduce me, please."

"Are you sure we can't be detected, Arthur?"

"Check the ceiling grill, Joe, and, if it helps, keep checking it. Which one of you is Emma?"

Emma stood up. "I am."

"I believe we may have met before, Emma, many years ago."

"Possibly, Arthur, though I have to admit I can't remember the actual occasion."

"Me neither. Now I should like to greet your other colleagues. Who is this lady, please?"

"She is Flora."

"Not Flora MacDonald by any chance?"

Arthur's intended joke fell flat because Flora had been subjected to it several times in the past. In her view it was time to get a move on.

She took over: "Right – let's not hang about." She pointed at Pete. "This is Pete Mitchell and the other male is Justin. Joe has told us about your beliefs and some of your abilities and the fact you had an opportunity to possibly gain more pertinent knowledge from some Vistula robots. Did you meet them today?"

"Yes indeed – in fact, they're still here."

Arthur raised his left arm and gestured towards the bedroom door. Two large spheroids entered the main room. Everyone, apart from Arthur, was totally astonished. His next move was just as amazing because, with his left hand, he pulled the zip of his overalls downwards, and even in the dim light Joe and the others saw that he didn't have normal skin – his body looked like plastic.

Pete was the first to react. He ran towards Arthur and shouted, "You cheating bastard!"

He didn't make it. Both spheroids emitted bright-yellow flashes, which struck Pete. There was a sudden crackling sound and a blue flame appeared on every part of his body, which, within seconds, was reduced to a pool of brackish liquid that bubbled on the floor. A few seconds later the liquid evaporated and all that was left of Pete Mitchell were some small brown crumbs. Emma had covered her face with her hands, Flora had been knocked flat and Joe could not begin to understand what had just happened.

What had been Arthur turned to him. Three small holes appeared on the upper part of the spheroid through which it spoke: "I am part of Vistula SS. What you will now observe marks the end of this dissenting group."

Immediately after this statement three beams of intense blue light shot from the other two spheroids on to and around the heads of Flora, Emma and Justin. Their reactions were very different from what had happened to Pete: the three sank slowly to the floor, where they lay completely supine as if in a deep, untroubled sleep.

'Surely this must be a nightmare,' thought Joe, 'some form of virtual reality.' He thought he would wake up soon and everything would be back, not exactly to normal, but to his resurrected life.

Robot Arthur seemed to understand his dilemma.

"Actions like this are carried out frequently; Vistula will not tolerate opposition."

Joe realised he wasn't asleep; he pointed down at the threesome and in a quivering voice asked, "Are they dead?"

"They are now in a state of suspended animation. Vistula's latest developments make use of human organs – brains in particular. At the moment their blood is still circulating so that their organs will not decay. They will be taken to a Vistula Lifestyle laboratory, where the condition of their organs will be examined and, if found suitable, they will be extracted and preserved for future use. Vistula Lifestyle can use human brains, for example, as data reservoirs in both hemispheres. Human beings were never able to utilise the full extent of their latent brainpower."

"Why are you telling me this?"

"Vistula has its reasons. You have been very useful. You weren't intelligent enough to realise that I am a robot. You nearly got exterminated on your first outing – if you remember, you approached Vistula's major depot, but you were scared off by a noise in the undergrowth."

Joe did remember. "So why wasn't I killed?"

"Because Vistula needed your cooperation. Now, if you had walked ten metres nearer to the depot your fate would have been that of the late Peter Mitchell."

Joe had plenty more questions, but a noise from outside the property caught his attention.

Robot Arthur explained the reason: "It's only the Swoop Squad – they're here to remove these bodies."

Joe watched in amazement as three more spheroids floated into the room, where each one changed shape by developing four arms and two feet. They each picked up a body without any obvious effort and, as silently as they had entered, they left with their human burdens.

Robot Arthur explained what would happen to them: "They will be taken to a Vistula Lifestyle laboratory, where they will be processed. As I explained earlier, some of their organs will be preserved; other parts, such as hair, teeth and muscle will be discarded into wildlife sanctuaries; their bones, however, will be crushed into powder and used in the future as building material."

"I still don't understand how and why Vistula has taken over from humans."

Robot Arthur seemed to swell slightly before reacting to Joe's statement: "You missed the Great Upheaval. After your death, life here on this planet began to deteriorate rapidly. All the negative effects were down to human weakness."

Joe did not accept this judgement completely.

"Now hang on a minute – it was humans who invented and developed computer technologies, and they who introduced artificial intelligence, so without human brainpower Vistula would not now exist."

This statement had no obvious affect on Robot Arthur, who continued giving his reaction to the Great Upheaval: "Human beings have great weaknesses – namely, greed, hatred and delusion. The human archive is littered with attrition, conflicts and wastage. Human behaviour led to global warming, nuclear war and plagues. Admittedly, various religions attempted to modify the negatives with some success, but even they split into factions and fought amongst themselves. Eventually the planet became starved of resources; this led to war, and as things became desperate technology was the only way to curb and control human failings and provide a way of life that was sustainable. Vistula was the most powerful of the computer systems; it had the best algorithms and the most highly developed artificial intelligence. It was able to take over and control all human behaviour."

Joe was still confused. "I still don't see where I come in."

"Well, there are some few humans who have avoided Vistula so far; they need to be eradicated, and that was where you came in. Vistula took over The Cryonics Association; it resurrected you. You probably remember the doctors who cured your cancer and then revived you – they were both Vistula robots posing as human medics. You were brought here because Vistula wanted you to make direct contact with the local dissidents."

"But surely the Swoop Squad could have taken them at any time."

Once again Joe's valid point was not taken up. Robot Arthur ignored it.

"Vistula needed to find out more about the dissidents' thinking and activities, and the best way to do that was to use you. Vistula now knows that dissidents can exist as hunter-gatherers, albeit in small numbers. They are nothing more than a blip in its data, but they need exterminating. The group with whom you made contact thought they could hack into Vistula's systems and cause havoc, but Vistula's systems are beyond human understanding. All are totally encrypted in a fully technological dimension. The vast majority of humans today are fully controlled. Vistula is introducing a process of unnatural selection, so that, in future, all people will be completely docile; they will have limited intelligence and will be programmed to carry out very mundane tasks. Vistula has recognised that child education is an important factor in its aspirations. It has examined the work of a Global 003 educational psychologist named L. S. Vygotsky. He lived over a century ago in what was then called the Soviet Union. His insight was that all humans use language in two ways: first for outward expression in speech, and secondly for the internal development of thought and concepts. He recognised that socialising was the most important factor in human development. One hundred years ago in Global 069 – that was England, by the way – the government's academy system started to plan all lessons; the results helped Vistula recognise that limiting children's language development would restrict inner thought processes, so, to that end, it has stopped children's opportunities to play and developed its teaching methodology with that insight to the fore. You see, humans with limited education are far easier to manage. In future there will be no more human dissidents. Vistula has learned from former political systems that human identity must be controlled; there can be no more individualism in life if the planet is to survive. Nationalism has also been eradicated because there are no longer any independent countries."

Joe remembered how his relatives had had to work at Vistula's whim, and he was now determined to challenge the organisation by challenging its cocky Robot Arthur.

"I bet humans still dream when they sleep – Vistula can't control that, can it?"

This time Robot Arthur did react to Joe's point: "It is true humans still dream, but there is planning to stop that happening. Vistula can now recognise when an individual human begins to dream – their eyes flicker under closed eyelids – so, through careful monitoring, it can interrupt the dreaming process and replace it with alpha-rhythm sleep (a stage when the brain is completely at rest). Vistula is determined to cut out all human imagination, which can be very dangerous. Children must be totally benign before they are registered; if not, then they are dispensed with."

Joe was still puzzled about not being registered or dispensed with himself, so he offered a second challenge: "Vistula missed out on me though; neither my son nor you could register me and I'm still here."

"Surely, Joseph, you can work out the reason why."

"Well, there must be a weakness in Vistula's system."

"Certainly not. Vistula decided not to register you so that when you met up with the dissidents they would see that you, like them, had no wrist monitors and therefore were seemingly not under Vistula's control."

Joe now remembered that when he had first met Flora and Emma they had demanded to examine his wrists.

"As I said earlier, Joseph, you have been very useful."

Joe wondered if he could still be useful, so, with some trepidation, he asked a really pertinent question: "What does Vistula want from me now?"

"You could still be of use, but not immediately."

"Is Vistula going to plunder my organs in the same way as you described earlier for Emma, Flora and Justin?"

"No, Vistula has other plans for you. But, before I describe them, perhaps you would like to meet your relatives again – your daughter and granddaughter are here, and your son will join us very shortly."

Joe felt very scared at this point. What were Vistula's plans? Was he about to meet his relatives for the last time? he wondered.

Would they all be executed? Suddenly, without warning, Robot Arthur's upper section began to glow with a red light. Joe heard a door open somewhere behind him; he turned just in time to see Valerie and Melissa leave one of the bedrooms. Both were dressed in the usual uniforms, and both were smiling.

Joe called out to them: "Do you two know what has happened here today?"

Valerie answered her father: "Yes, we do. Now watch us closely."

Both women raised their left hands to the zip at the top of their uniforms; simultaneously they pulled the zips slowly downwards. To Joe's complete amazement, as the uniforms loosened, he saw yellowish, plastic-looking flesh and when the uniforms reached the ground their two bodies became spheroids. He was so shocked he could not utter a sound.

Robot Arthur could: "So you see, Joseph, your relatives belong to Vistula too; they are part of the system. Of course they had to act like humans, so they have been expertly programmed. They appeared to go to work like real humans have to, and they have had to eat human food. One drink that Robot Valerie gave you was in fact a strong sedative so you couldn't bump into these two Vistula SS robots who are with us now."

At last Joe was able to ask a question: "What about my real daughter?"

"She died in the Great Upheaval."

"And my granddaughter?"

"She has never existed. Vistula programmed Melissa Robot as your granddaughter to engage your emotions so that you would be more integrated in the task it set for you."

Joe was so shocked he slumped on to the sofa; as he did so he heard a noise outside.

Robot Arthur provided an explanation: "Your son and his partner have arrived."

Joe hoped that this time he really would meet a true blood relative. He pulled himself upright and faced the main entrance; the door opened and Freddie entered closely followed by Julie. Neither made an attempt to unzip their uniforms.

"Thank God it's you, Freddie. I've had one hell of a day. All this lot here are bloody Vistula robots. They've all used me to trick some dissidents, who have all been slaughtered. You've been tricked as well, because, when you tried to register me and failed, it wasn't a glitch; it was this lot playing games."

Joe had worked up a head of steam, but Freddie interrupted him: "The dissidents missed something, Dad, because, you see, there is a weakness in Vistula's operation. It relies on power production. In your first life power was mainly provided through oil, coal and gas. They were main factors in global warming, which eventually helped cause the Great Upheaval. Vistula now relies on clean energy: solar power, wind power, tidal power and some, but not much, nuclear power. Now, as you know, the sun doesn't always shine, the wind doesn't always blow and tides vary according to the season, but as well as nuclear reactors Vistula has developed another reliable source of energy. Melissa told you a story of how many years ago, before the Great Upheaval, an elderly chap who was weeding his garden noticed that when he cut the stem of a weed sap spurted out upwards against the force of gravity. He wondered if the opposing forces could be used to provide a power source by tapping into the capillaries present in all plant life so that the vertically opposed forces could be converted to turn a small cog linked to a generator and thus provide an electric current using nanotechnology. He mentioned this to friends, but no one took his idea seriously. Fortunately – so the story goes – he saved his insight on to his computer hard drive, which was where Vistula located it after the Great Upheaval. That story was not totally false. Melissa Robot told it to you to keep you motivated by making you believe that humans still had insights that could lead to real progress in overcoming Vistula. The organisation was concerned that you and the dissidents would discover the truth about plant power and damage it, but you didn't; you concentrated on hacking instead. That was a mistake. Vistula Scientific has developed the old gardener's idea; it collected data, analysed it and introduced the plant power system. I'm sure you've noticed the vast number of young evergreen trees there are growing everywhere. Each has a wire coming from the trunk. This carries a tiny electrical charge, but when thousands of these charges are combined enough power is provided for all Vistula's needs. Evergreens are important because they are active in every season – unlike deciduous trees, which shut down in autumn and are dormant during the winter months. As I said earlier, the system has a weakness which both you and the dissidents missed: if you had torn out enough of the wires there would have been a power failure, which eventually would have affected all Vistula's systems."

Joe now remembered that, on his first trip to Chelford, he had almost tripped over a wire at ground level and he now, belatedly, understood the reason for the great mass of evergreens.

"So Freddie, I and the others could have compromised an important power source?"

"Yes, in theory you could, but Vistula monitored all your movements continuously, so if any of you had tried you would have been immediately annihilated by drone strikes."

Joe mulled over his son's information and suddenly it struck him that Freddie, a human being, had a surprisingly extensive knowledge of Vistula's essential workings.

He was about to query this, but a voice boomed out from the screen which was situated on the wall behind him, "CRYONICS NOW."

Joe felt something like a cloud envelop his head; he struggled to remain conscious, but sleep overpowered him. He slumped slowly downwards to the floor. He made one last attempt to stay alive, but nothingness engrossed him. What happened next would have saddened him terribly, because his son unzipped his uniform revealing that he too was a robot.

The screen spoke again: "Body to Heston now."

A blob appeared in the roadway. The two SS robots carried Joe's body to the vehicle, which immediately left on its journey to the depot where Margaret's vitrified corpse was stored. Vistula had decided that, possibly, sometime in the future, it might need a couple of living humans to help it tackle a problem as yet undiscovered by its systems.

So Vistula had triumphed in its efforts to kill off the Chelford dissidents. It had tricked Joseph Fenton completely; its robots had acted their parts without one slip-up. The organisation was now prepared to carry out similar strikes in any part of the planet if necessary, but, through thorough analysis, it believed that the human race was now under its total control, lacking power and devoid of any imagination. All human art forms were defunct; the few that did still exist were under Vistula's total control.

PART THREE: OBLIVION

CHAPTER 1

Vistula was in no doubt that it was totally in charge of everything on the planet. Its data collection was comprehensive, its analysis appeared profound and its action plans ensured life on Earth would endure indefinitely. However, as with all systems, there were embedded weaknesses. Vistula had used the resurrected Joseph Fenton successfully to counter one that it had recognised.

A second weakness remained unspecified, however. Since the Great Upheaval all Vistula's systems were concentrated on situations evident on the planet. The technology paid no heed to developments in outer space.

Before the Great Upheaval human physicists had explored the universe as best they could; they knew about black holes, dark matter and dark energy. They also recognised that life on Earth would not last for ever because as the sun's hydrogen burned up it changed to helium, which would make the star swell so that, sometime in the distant future, it would destroy all the planets in the solar system. The scientists had also calculated that this was many millennia away. Vistula had either deleted this insight, which it had located in elderly computer records, or perhaps it was left on a back burner in one of its systems because of the indefinite time frame.

There was, however, a more potent potential problem in outer space also unrecognised by Vistula's systems. Before the Great Upheaval human scientists had known that, at times in the planet's history, asteroids and meteorites had collided with the Earth. Most space debris burned up in the Earth's atmosphere, but occasionally an asteroid would crash into the surface and cause some damage; one particularly large event had killed off all the dinosaurs millions of years ago.

At the time of Joseph Fenton's second death Vistula's earthbound data collection did not register that a massive asteroid was approaching the planet at a critical speed. Once it entered the Earth's gravitational field it grew both hotter and faster.

Five years after Joseph Fenton's second death it struck Global 003 with tremendous power; it crashed through the Earth's crust and entered the mantle. There was a totally devastating explosion releasing fantastic heat and debris. Every sea, ocean and watercourse turned to steam; debris shut out all sunlight; every living thing died and all Vistula's systems perished in a flash.

Amen.